THE
VAMPIRE STATE

THE
VAMPIRE
STATE

The Secret Lives of Las Vegas Vampires &

The Rise of Harold Halbmann

JAMES R. HINDS

TATE PUBLISHING
AND ENTERPRISES, LLC

Published by Tate Publishing & Enterprises, LLC
127 E. Trade Center Terrace | Mustang, Oklahoma 73064 USA
1.888.361.9473 | www.tatepublishing.com

Tate Publishing is committed to excellence in the publishing industry. The company reflects the philosophy established by the founders, based on Psalm 68:11,
"The Lord gave the word and great was the company of those who published it."

Book design copyright © 2014 by Tate Publishing, LLC. All rights reserved.
Cover design by Anne Gatillo
Interior design by Jomel Pepito

Published in the United States of America

ISBN: 978-1-63122-643-4
1. Fiction / Fantasy / Contemporary
2. Fiction / Romance / Paranormal
14.06.16

To My Readers

While I attempted to incorporate something of the atmosphere of Las Vegas and Nevada in this work I have not drawn any of the characters or incidents in this novel from any real individuals or occurrences. In other words, this novel is a work of imagination, a piece of pure fiction, and its characters and their deeds should be viewed as such.

VAMP QUEST '09

I. FIRST BLOOD

Not long ago, in 2009, there was an old man who lived in Las Vegas, retired after a career of many years of government service. He had seen seventy-five years and lived alone, except for his dog and a cat. He stood five foot seven, weighed 184 pounds, and had a potbelly. He had always weighed about the same, but at sixty-five, his paunch had suddenly appeared as if by magic, and his buttocks, formerly substantial, now had dimples on either side. He dressed simply most days in khakis, guayabera shirts, plain gray or black socks, and leather loafer shoes. On Sundays, he spruced up a bit, wore his best clothes, and took his mother who lived around the corner to church.

His gray stucco house had a living-dining room, a kitchen, a family room, and three bedrooms, one of which he had fitted out as a library. He had comfortable rather than elegant furniture—a couple of sofas, a stuffed chair, and plain chairs around the dining room table. He had a comfortable king-sized bed, a night stand, and for the guest room, a daybed. Also, the family room, the living room, and the library were full of shelves with countless books, most of them paperback novels—almost all of them about vampires. In fact, he spent most of his income on them, a paltry 900 dollars a month, including 50 from Social Security. (He had offsets, you see, lest he become incredibly wealthy from double-dipping!) For this reason, he also worked part-time as a library aide, returning books to the shelves and earning a few dollars more to keep himself from starvation.

Ernest Frank, that is his name. He had read almost every book about vampires, at least all of them in paperback. Many years ago, he had devoured Bram Stoker's *Dracula* and Polidore's work. (I won't even start on the movies about the undead he had seen.) More recently, he feasted on Anne Rice's *Interview with a Vampire* and her other books, Nancy Baker's *Kiss of the Vampire*, Lynsay Sands's *Single White Vampire*, and a vast number of other novels.

He started reading just as a lark, something to escape from the boredom and poverty in his life. He was educated as a historian, and he certainly knows the difference between fact and fiction and how to determine it. After writing history for the Air Force for thirty years, he was fired for wanting to tell the truth. (To be sure, they concealed the reason under a subterfuge—his histories were late, the same as everyone else's, and often had many typos since they always made sure he got the worst typists in the pool.). All of that came before everyone adopted computers, of course. He just wasn't paying enough attention when colonels told him, "We don't want to air our dirty linen." Later, he tried to publish his own work and found interesting topics to research, but his old bosses had written some of the journals, warning them not to touch anything of his, and since the military are a major market for those publications, they took the hint. Then too most commercial book companies were not interested in publishing about obscure unpublished military campaigns in distant lands. Also, academic publishers did not like books by has-beens who were not employed by their universities. They wanted to be the first to bring out the work of rising stars or at least to sustain the reputations of their own faculties. So what is the point of writing if nobody else cares?

What would it be like, he wondered, *if he could live for many centuries, and be a living witness and a historian for the events of such a period? He could write history such as no mortal ever could.* He could even say, *I too, was there and saw it with my own eyes!* Thus he became deeply involved in reading about vampires. Was there some core of truth from which these legends arose? He found a most interesting volume: Raymond T. McNally and Radu Florescu's *In Search of Dracula* (1972). The book contains some of the more or less similar legends about Dracula originally told in Romanian, Russian, and German. None of these deal directly with vampirism, and they just paint the picture of a cruel medieval warlord; another chapter deals with a Hungarian countess who killed girls to bathe in their blood.

What do the novels themselves tell us about Dracula? he pondered. Most early literature treats Dracula the vampire as a creature of the devil. He is entirely evil as are those he turns. The prince can be charming and even seductive, but then, in the nineteenth century, sex was itself evil, at least outside the narrow permitted zone of marriage. Everything was black and white in those days; homosexuals were evil too. Vampires, at least the males, had extraordinary powers, great strength, and they could turn into bats and other night creatures, but they were vulnerable to sunlight and to religious symbols such as the cross or holy water. Female vampires, not so strong, depended wholly on their seductive powers, or they feed on children, at least according to Stoker. Anne Rice and some others continue in the old tradition, with stronger feminine figures, but in today's permissive society, the image of the vampire seems to be changing. He or she is now either heroic or more a victim of misfortune than anything else.

Why is it that children, when they are six, are enthralled by dinosaurs, but by the time they are sixteen, at least the girls, they are thrilled by vampires? Is it because teenagers want to believe that they are immortal themselves? They throw themselves into life, ignoring its dangers and drive their cars like there was no tomorrow, and for some, there isn't. Is it the thrill of the out-of-this-world sexuality? There is just something marvelous about vampires, I think, something unfathomable. Do they really exist?

In more recent literature, vampires are often far less evil, and they can be heroes even. They don't drain every victim dry. They just use a feed-and-forget-me technique. That leaves their food free to go on its way, at least in most cases. Of course, there are still evil vampires who don't care, and often, vampires share their pages with other supernatural creatures such as werewolves, shape-shifters, ghouls, and zombies. In today's post-religious world, vampires are mostly atheists who care not a whit for the powers of holy water and crosses, although they still fear silver, the stake and the sun. Many no longer simply burn up in the sun, although most remain creatures of the night. Most don't sleep in coffins anymore or haunt cemeteries. In Sands's books, they are not even undead, but they are descendants of Atlantes or people of Atlantis. Others still regard them as pulseless and children of Cain. So what are they then, really?

Ernest wanted to know.

Once in a while, modern criminals have approached the ferocity of vampires, as for example, with the deeds of Richard Speck or Charles Manson's Tate-La Bianca killings. The Manson murderers wrote on a wall in blood, but they did not actually drink it. Or did they?

Trying to sort through all this is very, very confusing, and he hardly knew what to make of it. Reality is what we see, the evidence of our senses and of documents. Sometimes there are no documents, and our senses are limited, and fail us. Are fantasy and reality then sometimes really one and the same?

Is the imagined world real just because we can conceive it, or is the real world itself inconceivable? If vampires are real, maybe—just maybe—Ernest could find one and ask him. Sure, it will be dangerous to look for them, and really, he doesn't want to be killed for his blood or turned. What did he have to lose? He would only be missed by his mom, maybe by his faithful hound, Ralph, and his cat. (Hey, if he were ever turned, maybe he could visit his ex-employers at Randolph Air Force Base—but then, no.) No Christian should do anything but forgive his enemies, not nurse grievances.

Therefore, he decided to dedicate himself to the task of finding a vampire. I'll call his adventure Vamp Quest '09. What better, more decadent place to launch it than Las Vegas? The city's prosperity depends more and more on its nighttime entertainment so it's a place where vampires should thrive—a great hunting ground. Well, maybe an older city like New Orleans would be slightly better, but for budgetary reasons, a trip over there would have to wait.

The best way to start, he reasoned, was with a survey of the nightlife in Las Vegas clubs and casinos. There, he could keep an eye out for unusually pale or unusually flushed (from recent feeding) folks lining up to get into the hotspots or for girls who showed the tell-tale punctures of vampire canines above their skimpy tops. He could ensure his personal protection (maybe) by wearing a silver cross on a chain since even atheist vampires might fear silver, and he would carry a water pistol filled with holy water, a solid wooden stake, and a metal worker's hammer. In addition, he would wear a necklace made of garlic cloves just in case. He would also slip a small Gideons's *New Testament* in his suit pocket for a little extra-scriptural power. Then the whole adventure would be fun even if he never found a vampire, and his mother would be happy he was going out instead of spending all his time writing or with his nose buried in a book.

Vamp Quest '09 would involve definite sacrifices as well. He would have to cut way back on his purchases of new paperbacks because he would need more money for cleaning and pressing his best clothes used only for wearing to church. He might even need a little money for some new, more fashionable clothes. Not too much, though. Books are way more important than raiment. Also, he would have to have money for the clubs.

Having laid his plans, he went into the bathroom carrying *Interview with the Vampire*, closed the door, as was his custom, pulled down his pants and sat on the toilet, and opened the book to the part where the characters are in Paris, and he began to read the place where the characters are in the *Théâtre des Vampires*. Then, he noticed something. A furry paw was thrust under the door, which creaked as it was pulled outward. When the door opened, there was Sandy, his cat, with an expression that seemed to say "What on earth are you doing in there?"

"Pervert," he said with a laugh and pushed the door back closed with his foot. Sandy was so darn curious that whenever he took a shower, she climbed up on the window ledge to watch him. And she always paraded around to be seen if a guest came. Strangely, she and Ralph were pals.

Another phase of his plan, he decided, would to be to keep an eye on the foreclosed and empty houses that were all too common in Las Vegas nowadays. Maybe vampires hid out there during the daytime since they were perfect for that. He didn't intend to go there to stake anyone. He really just wanted to ask questions, not to persecute. Any weapons he would carry would be just for self-defense, just as he might do around the more dangerous members of his own kind.

Vampires, he thought, surely would look for areas where most houses were empty, and they would probably prefer the more luxurious houses, not the derelict homes on the west side frequented by the homeless people, drug addicts, and the like. They might go there for a meal or two, but they would prefer quiet during the day so they would remain undisturbed. Still the night club scene offered the safest chance for an interview since it would be hard to kill you in a room full of people without attracting notice.

Two weeks' research produced no results for him. At the Platinum Club, a long line of guys and scantily dressed women waited to get in. Ernest waited an hour, and although dressed in his best Sunday clothes and despite offering five dollars to the doorman, he couldn't get in. All the man said was, "You've got to be kidding," after looking him over with a dismissive glance. At least, he got a chance to observe the girls who showed no visible fang marks, although several had tattoos. Ernest did manage to get into the New York Club and Risqué after he discovered fifty dollars was more effective than five. Again, most of the women had bare shoulders and throats, quite a few tattoos, and no fang marks. In general, the club-goers, especially the younger girls, looked at Ernest as if he were from Mars.

At Quartier Latin, a Parisian-themed night club, disaster struck. Ernest didn't find any people with puncture marks on their throats, and in fact, one girl who misinterpreted his looking at her neck for looking down her cleavage actually slapped him. "You pervert!" she said, and Ernest turned away quickly. Very embarrassing! He fled the scene at once.

He returned another day and got into the club but found nothing. Most young people waiting to start a hot night of partying just laughed at him, at that strange old guy, in his square out-of-fashion clothing.

Even Ernest's visit to the vampire-themed club Fangs was a bust. Mostly, they just had strippers with fake fangs dressed in scanty outfits doing burlesque routines on stage. A few of the girls attending were dressed in dark clothing with pierced nostrils and even lips instead of necks, but that was all. Really, it was nothing that unusual for Las Vegas.

At night, he tried patrolling, driving his old Taurus along the streets to see if he could detect unusual activity that might prove vampires were there. If there were vampires sleeping in repossessed homes, they must have been hanging out in gated communities. Perhaps Las Vegas was not such a good place for vampires after all. If Paris, France, used to be the City of Light back then, today, Las Vegas fits the description better. The sun-filled days of an almost perpetual summer (spring starts in February, fall comes in November, and winter is a little hiccup between late December and mid-January) are but a preface to its neon-lighted nights. A city that never sleeps, that also fits. It is also a town for every pleasure known to man, legal or not.

The casino empire that is Las Vegas can be divided into three zones—the traditional strip; Las Vegas Boulevard, with its high-rise high-roller resorts; the downtown, or Freemont Street

Experience, long favored by less affluent locals and new resorts, along Rampart, Rancho, and elsewhere, often built despite the objections of nearby residents who later flock to their movie theaters, ice rinks, and bowling alleys. (Las Vegas belongs to its casino and construction industries. Everyone else can go to hell, thank you!)

Then, Ernest's big break came when behind the Flames of Love nightclub at around two in the morning. The feeble light of a single lamp encased in a metal cage, illuminated their faces just a little more clearly than the moonlight. He stepped back into the shadow of the foul-smelling Dumpster, forgetting that vampires can see just as well in the dark as in light, but fortunately, the creature's attention was fixed on the girl. This young man had his fangs deep in the neck of a hot, scantily dressed girl, whose thigh-high minidress plunged to her navel and barely hung on her shoulders, revealing most of her neck, shoulders, and breasts. She clung to her gold lame purse even while her life was draining away. Then he pulled back, cut himself on the hand with a pocket knife, and held his hand so that a thin stream of blood fell into her half-opened mouth. The girl finally collapsed, and the vampire picked her up easily and carried her to a parked van, opened the door, and threw her inside. Then he returned to gather up her purse and tossed it inside the vehicle before closing the door. Finally, he went back to the rear exit of the casino and entered it.

Ernest waited a few moments, then followed, determined to corner the monster, and ask him a few questions. Inside, where there were people, he reasoned, it would be safer. The guy was just a little way down the hall, and there were a few other people but some distance away.

Gathering up his courage and thinking fast, he said, "Sir, I don't think you closed the door of your van very well. Also, you better move it from the handicapped zone before the police ticket you."

The vampire whirled with a hiss and flashed his fangs. "Just leave me alone, and maybe I'll let you live."

Ernest caught the red glow of his eyes but quickly fixed his own on the floor, so the vampire couldn't mesmerize him and held up his cross before himself. "I don't want you to do that, nor will I want to hurt you. Just kidding about the parking, but I want to talk with you. Let's go into the coffee shop."

When Ernest had settled into a somewhat isolated booth of a nearby coffee shop he addressed the vampire, who seemed to be a young man of about twenty-five, six feet tall, with a somewhat florid complexion, a wiry blond hair, dressed in a short-sleeved shirt, tie, slacks, and Doc Martins. "My name is Ernest, I want to know who you are, how you became a vampire, what you do, and all about your life."

"I could never tell you that and let you live."

"What does it matter what you accomplish if no one knows about it? If Achilles himself had not found a Homer, his tomb would have buried him, and his name would have perished forever. I, though a mere mortal, can make you and your kind more immortal than even eternal life. Let me be your biographer or historian," he said, looking down at the table between them. "I can change some names, and no one will be able to find you to get revenge, but all the world will hear of your exploits."

A moment of silence passed.

"One thing only," Ernest added. "I must have the truth, for anything else is worthless. Our craft demands it, depends on it, and is valued and measured by it."

"We immortals are creatures of the shadows, and if the world knew we were more than a legend, they would destroy us," the vampire said.

"Not if what I write is truthful yet still conceals your identity," Ernest said. "But people could know what it is like to be a vampire. So how is it you became one? What is the vampire community like, especially here, in Las Vegas?" Ernest took out a small tape recorder and a note book.

"Let's call me Richard York," the vampire said. "I used to come here several times a year from New York to *play*, if you know what I mean. I was still single. This time, it was early, and I was having a great time in town, enjoying the themed resorts, from volcanoes to dancing waters, but was not ready for serious gaming or clubbing. There were these people who thrust papers with raunchy photos of local hookers at you. A couple of the girls were not bad looking, but you never know what you might catch that way. One guy, however, who looked a little shabby, pale, and worn out, no doubt some alcoholic, was handing out flyers for nightclubs. A couple of them were a little unusual. One was the Flames of Love with a live band, where you come to drink, dance, and sin, and single hot girls get in free—presumably someone at the door decided who was hot enough—and then there was the Bordello Club, where there was a great band, the most beautiful women in Las Vegas, an all-night party, and hot single guys could come free. Now I had never heard of a club that would do that. They all want sexy girls to come so as to attract men who would pay. Was this some kind of gay club? Well, they did claim to have the best-looking women in town, and that seemed to refute that idea.

"The Bordello turned out to be a great club. When I got there, the guy at the door sent me straight in where I found the floor filled with gyrating dancers, the women in outfits that left little to the imagination, and the music so loud that you could hear little conversation. As the name suggests, the club was brothel themed, and a couple of the girls even took off their tops. The managers paid no attention. The place was smoking! I headed to the bar to fortify myself with a couple of drinks before looking for someone to hook up with.

"Her name was Delia, and I have to admit, she was one of the most beautiful girls I have ever laid eyes on. She was around twenty-five, with blond hair, blue eyes, and a super figure. She had natural breasts I could see clearly through the transparent top of her minidress. I asked her for a dance, and she told me a little about herself, including that she was a year around resident in town. After a couple of dances, she suggested we go to her place. Even after a few drinks, I was ready but a little apprehensive. She sensed it and said, 'Don't worry. I'll treat you just like one of my family.'

"Her room was nice, and we had a view of the strip. We sat down on the sofa and after a little kissing and touching, I reached around for the zipper of her dress. 'Okay?' I asked, looking into her eyes. 'Oh, yeah!' she said. As she was taking off her dress, she suddenly said, 'Ouch!' There was a pin, and I've pricked myself, and she held up her bloody thumb. 'Would you kiss it and make it all better?' I did that, of course, and once we had stripped, I kissed her lips and throat and breasts. Then I entered her, and suddenly, I felt a sharp pain, then a feeling of bliss, and drifted off. Then, I had a nightmare of suffering pain, chills, and nausea. 'Damn it,' I thought then. 'I must have had way too much booze. How could I miss this wonderful moment?'

"When I awoke, light was already coming in under the drawn shade over the window. *I need to get back to my room*, I thought. *But I need to apologize to Delia for flunking out on her that way.* Since I didn't see her, I pulled my clothes back on and threw open the door to the room. The light was blinding, and suddenly, I felt way too weak and staggered back into the room.

"Then I saw Delia coming toward me. 'Don't go out,' she said. 'Just stay here with me.' I said, 'All of my stuff is over in my motel. I'm sorry I was so drunk.'

"Then she replied, 'If you really want it, you can pick it up tomorrow evening, but right now, you need to sleep. You were great. You have a new life here now and a new job. We're expanding the Bordello Club and expanding our operations, and we want you to work at the Flames of Love to recruit us some fine new girls. You'll have all the food you want, good action, and money, besides. You were way too cute to dump down some mine shaft. You're part of my family now.'

"Then a smile spread across Delia's face, revealing her perfect white teeth and two real fangs. 'Welcome to our family,' she said, and with that, I realized that my life had changed forever."

"I've heard all new vampires are crazy for blood, almost uncontrollable," Ernest inquired, "Is that true?"

"Delia kept me there for about a week and helped me collect my things. She also taught me I didn't always have to kill my food. I could just drink a little at times, although it is often just as good to simply kill the victim and dump him in the desert. It saves the work of convincing the person he or she had never met a vampire and had only experienced a nightmare. Certain people we save and turn to support our operations."

"So Delia supplied you with food that week?"

"The first were some Mexican or Central American maids who very much wanted to keep their jobs and seemed to understand that their lives also depended on their silence. If one of them had gone to the police, we could have denied the story and said she was only unhappy because the club had discovered she was an illegal immigrant and fired her. They preferred to lose a little blood and keep on working for the club instead of being deported or even killed. They are even better than some of the Goth types that hang out at Fang and actually want to be bitten. We don't have to mesmerize them either."

"What did you tell your employer, family, and friends?" said Ernest.

"Right now, nothing. Later, they will learn that I died."

"So that is how vampires handle things. They just become missing persons or fabricate stories about their own deaths. Isn't it sad to lose contact with all your family and friends?"

"It is, but it is far better than having them think you've become a monster. And in the first days of your new condition, you need a lot of blood and could be a real danger to them as well."

"Why do you need so much blood at the start?" Ernest asked.

"Remember, when you're turned, the vampire who does that drinks almost all of your blood and puts just a small amount of his own blood back, just enough to start the conversion. You must have enough to continue the transformation. Once you stabilize, you don't need as much."

Ernest wanted to know many more things about the vampire world, and how much of this was exactly true, but he realized that Richard had things to do, and dawn would be upon them very soon.

"Amazing! Richard, I want to meet you again. Tomorrow at the same time if possible and learn even more about the vampire world and especially about Las Vegas."

"If you let me check over what you write, I could talk to you more, but if you reveal our identities or information that would make them clear, I would have to kill you for sure. So if you show me what you intend to publish, you will be safe…for now."

"Yes, I understand," said Ernest.

"Otherwise, I have to erase it all, and if I can't, I'll kill you."

"Yes. Good night then. Oh, what will happen to the girl?"

"Tomorrow, she will awake to a new life and a new job. She was already half a vampire. Now she will really be one totally."

"If she doesn't want to do that?" Ernest asked. He wanted to know.

"She dies then. I don't believe that will happen, but it's possible. So long then, until tomorrow. Same time, same place."

As he strode briskly away, Ernest wondered if he would really keep his appointment and truly reveal the hidden world of the vampires, or if even trying to discover it would mark himself for death. So he returned home to his own life, his dusty books, his mom, his dog, and his cat.

Censorship seemed to always be part of his life, he mused, *first from the Air Force and now by a vampire.*

II. Vampirism 101

Ernest was already seated in the security of the same booth when Richard came in. Richard took a seat across from Ernest and tried to fix his gaze upon the mortal's face. Ernest greeted him and quickly looked away and around the room.

"What is it like being a vampire?" Ernest asked.

"Being a vampire is a lot different than most humans would imagine," Richard claimed. "People think vampires live forever. They are *dead*. They wake up every evening and ravage humanity to drink blood. You are invincible if you stay away from people carrying sharp stakes. No problems, right? No, not quite. Delia initiated me into her family, as she put it, and took some pains to explain what I had to do to survive my metamorphosis. 'Don't forget I made you,' she said, 'and I want to make sure that you stay around for a long, long time.'

"I asked, 'You mean you're my sire?' She answered, 'Does anything about me look at all masculine?' I said no, and I didn't need a second glance. 'I'm your mistress,' she said, 'and I mean that in both senses of the word. Our relationships are different, however, from those of humans. I fully expect, no want, no plan for you to have relations with other females. With vampires, that's a given. Whenever I want you, want to be with you, to spend the night, or for any other reason, I will summon you, and you will come.'

"She gave me a few simple survival tips, advising me never to tell any human what I was, unless I would kill him or her immediately after with no exceptions. Also, if anyone learns about me, I was to kill him or her. If, however, someone I have feelings for discovers the truth, then I could set up the person to turn. The newbie has to accept things then, or I would still have to dispose of her or him.

"She told me what I needed to know about myself. We are not undead at all. Our metabolism is just lower than that of a Galapagos tortoise when we are sleeping or hibernating. Mortals think we are dead, but we don't decay because we are alive.

Everything is just so slow as to be undetectable. We must eat at least twice or at the least once every week to stay active. We can consume human food, but it won't do the job. Only blood will. If we don't feed, we will spiral down and go into hibernation, which we might not ever come out of."

"What is the origin of vampires?" Ernest asked.

"Delia told me we are an ancient race that came from a distant planet many million years ago, then crossbred with humans. The ability of immortals to sleep centuries even and consume little energy in that state helped them to transverse the vast distances between worlds, distances men measure in light years. She pointed out the evidence. The Egyptian *Book of the Dead* talks of going back and forth out of the body in the tomb. It is why they worked so hard to preserve the physical remains of the dead. Of course, not all were vampires, but some were. Anyway, Delia explained what I would be doing now that she had turned me.

"She told me I was going to work at the Flames of Love, where I was assigned to recruit us the hottest of hot young women, seducing them, bedding them, turning them, or killing and disposing of them. 'Pick the prettiest girls,' she said, 'in the skimpiest clothes because they make the best recruits, with a little less pride than others.' No chemicals though. They have to give themselves willingly, to invite you in. I just need to get only a couple a week, and I will get all the sex I want and drink my fill. The ones we keep, I must offer a glass of wine first, wine laced with my blood before I drink from them. Otherwise, I have to cut my hand and dribble blood down their throats right afterward. The virus in my blood multiplies fast and attaches itself to every cell in their bodies.

"Richard asked Delia about whores. 'Better yet,' she had replied. 'Those women are already more than half vampires, so they make the change easier. Just one thing, whatever girl you change has to accept her new life, or we will have to dispose of her. Please don't send us many of those. Let each girl know she can have all the handsome guys, never worry about birth control since we ovulate only once every hundred years, and believe me, 'we always know when.' A woman vampire in heat has a raging sexual desire for her lover, be he a vampire or mortal. 'And men's blood is so sweet, as is yours my love,' Delia said. But I have to make sure my targets come to the club alone. Very rarely we can take two hot women, but in general, I should avoid targeting those who bring a friend.

"Once I drink more than eight ounces of blood, I must take all of their blood, or else, they die a horrible death. My saliva will tranquilize them for a while, but if they wake up, they can't eat. Their stomachs can't hold anything down, they toss and turn in agony, and eventually, their heart or lungs fail. She advised me to kill with kindness and to stop drinking when their hearts stop, if it were already too late.

"I shouldn't kill too many either. Vampires are friends of humans. We cull and purify the race, taking out the suicidal loners and leaving happy family members alone. We need them. They are our food, our drink. Also, we can't just dump bodies all over the neighborhood or let things at the club get too out of hand. The club would lose its liquor license. When necessary, our disposal squad takes remains out into the desert.

"'You'll like your first party,' Delia had said. 'You won't even have to tell a single lie to them.' Then Delia flashed me that smile or hers, her sensual lips parting to reveal the fangs that had transformed my life."

"You have an extraordinary memory for details," said Ernest. "So was the other night your first party?"

"No, I have been a vampire now for over a year."

"Doesn't it bother you killing helpless people just to feed your blood lust?"

"Mostly I avoid that," Richard said. "I either take only a little blood and mesmerize them, so they think they had a nightmare, or I transform them for the club and for other vampire requirements."

"What kind of requirements?" Ernest wanted to know.

"Well, beside girls to act as decoys attracting men to clubs, others are required for work at the sex ranches just outside Clark County."

"Really, are most brothel prostitutes really vampires?"

"No, but a few are. And those few are among the best. First, they gain experience, but they never age. They can't transmit diseases, and don't have to use birth control. They do but only because it's legally required. Also, they don't have pimps, sometimes human pets but never pimps."

"I can see it would really be dangerous to try to abuse a vampiress," Ernest said.

"A few pimps have sought to recruit our girls," said Richard with pride, "but the first time they attempt to bully or abuse them, these guys simply disappear. It's exactly the opposite of what usually happens with humans."

"So the vampire world has few problems?"

"I wouldn't say that exactly," Richard noted. "Just as in the human world, politics can be a real problem."

"I'd like to know more about that, Richard," said Ernest. "Tomorrow night, I'm busy, but I would like to meet you Thursday to hear more and show you some of my draft story about Vegas Vampires."

So Ernest went home again to work on his manuscript, read more about vampires, help his mother, and feed his dog and cat. Vamp Quest '09 seemed to promise really interesting things.

Just what questions should I ask next time? Ernest mused.

III. The Vegas Vampire Crisis

Ernest sat down in the half-deserted coffee shop and waited half an hour. Richard was late. Would he actually come again and tell more fascinating things?

Richard did come and sat down across from him, looked over at him, and shook his head.

"What is going on with vampire operations these days?" Ernest asked.

"Weird things. Three months ago, the Bordello Club was only beginning to fill up when I arrive to look for Delia. She had requested me to join her for the first time in three weeks for a business meeting, she said. I made my way into the room where cocktail waitresses dressed in skimpy tops and daisy dukes, body suits or baby dolls circulated with trays of drinks. Delia looked exactly as I had last seen her.

"'Well, hello, Rich!' she said and smiled but revealed nothing of her true nature. 'Big things have been happening around here and we need to talk.' I'd heard rumors, but I couldn't see how anything I'd heard would change what I'd been doing."

"Delia said she had plans that would mean a big opportunity for me, my brothers, and my ladies. Then she asked me what I had heard. I told her that the King of Vampires and the Las Vegas Satrap are going after the strip clubs in Las Vegas and the brothels in Nye County. The King wanted to be sure and get his royal fifth of the revenue, but the Satrap was claiming because of the expenses involved it should just be a tenth.

"It would involve me because when we expanded, she wanted me to manage one of the gentlemen's clubs or a brothel. There was much we had to do first, lining up support on the county commission to secure licensing and so on. A lot of money was needed, and some of our girls, among them was the stunning Julia, were to help us convert certain brothel owners to our cause. She observed with a smile. Since most were bachelors or divorced, they would be able to do so unnoticed. The clubs would be a harder proposition, but their own corruption and misconduct would open the door if we could learn the details. She instructed me to brief my girls—Julia, Georgia, Emily, and Bree—on the details she explained."

"Who are Julia, Georgia, Emily, and Bree?" Ernest asked.

"They are my daughters, so to speak. I am their sire," the vampire responded.

"You turned them?"

"Exactly so."

"One of them was the girl I saw you with that first night?"

"That was Bree. Anyway, Julia wasn't too crazy about the idea at first. She required some convincing."

Richard had asked her how her life at the Bordello Club was going. She was not happy that sometimes she had to kill and dispose of men.

"It's hard," she had said, "especially when I have to kill. I mean, at least I get to make a few immortals, but sometimes, it's awful. At least, they suffer no pain. I never believed I would do evil."

"Julie," Richard had told her, "you are no more evil than a lioness, a tigress, or a she-wolf. You are a killer by nature and always really were, really. I just brought out the vampire that was already within you. Actually, we help humans even if they are our food. You know that."

"You are always saying that, but it is still hard," Julia said. "At least, I get to keep some of the best guys, your grandsons. I would turn more if it were allowed, but we can't make too many."

"We have a special job for you and a great opportunity," promised Richard. "We want you for the Love Ranch, where you will work, and you won't need to kill anybody, hardly."

"As a hooker? No, thanks, that's just not me," Julia stated.

"Hear me out. If you undertake this plan, you will become one of the most powerful vampires in Nevada, maybe even in the country. Anyway, you never had problems having sex as a mortal, so why now?"

"It's different. I mean that was recreational, so it didn't really count except for prudes. This would be too…professional," Julia said, wrinkling her cute little nose.

"The main thing is not the clientele. We want you to become the girlfriend of John Strange and turn him. As his mistress, you can bring his business into our orbit, so to speak. It would also have this advantage for you. You could just feed from him rather than kill more guys. I think that would please you."

"It would, I believe. Don't they have cameras in every room? How would I handle that?"

"They are only concerned when you are negotiating money. They won't care if you draw a little blood, especially since you can heal the wounds. Mesmerize them, and they'll leave none the wiser."

"That would be okay, I guess. Once I turn Strange, I'll be queen there at any rate."

"You'll be our first at that place, and any others will be under your charge. Just keep them under control and make sure that not too many guys disappear, and it will work out really great for you," advised Richard.

"I told her that so that she would understand that I picked her as more experienced and better able to manage things so as to keep the ranch from becoming a center of suspicion. That and her natural inclinations of kindness should make her perfect for her role," Richard recalled later to Ernest.

"I was not prepared for the way things worked out so smoothly. John, that great bear of a man, all jolly and constantly joking with his girls, fell for her like a ton of bricks, and became one of ours. Our expansion of the strip clubs went into high gear, and we soon had vampire strippers who were a great part of the scene. The Clark County commissioners were fully as receptive to campaign contributions as those in Nye. There was no trouble licensing our new club, Nights of Passion.

"Money came rolling in very well, then a little less when the economy didn't rebound fast enough. Unfortunately, the Satrap of Nevada and the King of vampires didn't agree on the amounts that were to be their shares. I urged the Satrap to pay the extra cut, just to keep the peace, but he protested that it was excessive to the requirements of vampire law and the whole issue should go to the Vampire Guardians of Justice. I really wish that had happened.

"I had only been manager there for a week when one night, with the club packed, a huge explosion tore through the building. Fortunately, I had gone back to the office to deposit some of the proceeds into the safe. The whole building shook, and when I came out, everything was in chaos—girls screaming and the dead and mangled lying everywhere amid body parts. Pools of blood and shards of glass covered the area. Customers were panicking and trying to get out the exit. Just as many were out in front, a car blew up and flaming gasoline and pieces of metal decimated those who were fleeing. Over a hundred people—some vampires included—employees and customers were killed. Another two hundred or so of the humans had to be hospitalized.

"That night, the Satrap of Nevada disappeared, and six of his body guards turned up dead. Rumor has it that he and his two vampire guards were staked out somewhere in the desert."

"They just burst into flames and turned to ashes then?" asked Ernest.

"It wouldn't have been so easy for them as that. No, they just slowly burned black in the heat. Vampires don't explode in the sun, but they burn more easily than humans, and the results of long exposure like that are fatal."

"That was the end of my management role, at least for now. The new Satrap didn't kill me or anything, but he had his own supporters to reward. Never mind that I had urged our leader to go along with the King. It didn't matter. Vampire politics suck," he said with a sad shake of the head.

"I'll remember that," Ernest said. "Didn't the fire department say the cause was a gas leak, and the second explosion was caused when the blast set the car on fire? The Channel 13 television news and *Review-Journal* covered that story completely."

"Yeah, the vampire world knows how to grease the palms of humans to keep the truth about its activities from the public."

"And Julia?" Ernest wanted to know.

"She's still queen of the desert. Sometimes, I pretend to be a customer just to see her again. You know there's just something special about the first girl you turn."

"Doesn't John object to you fooling around with his girlfriend?"

"No, he's been initiated into our ways, which are different from yours. And Julie, she loves us both, but I am her sire, just as Delia will always be my mistress." Richard paused then said, "Now let us see what you have written about us."

Richard looked at Ernest's draft and nodded. After a few minutes, he said, "Take that name there and change it, and don't put into the story what Emily is doing now."

"Okay," Ernest said. "Consider it done."

Suddenly, Richard's eyes, huge and glowing red, were locked on his. Ernest couldn't draw away or reach for a weapon. He couldn't move. "Should I turn you now or just kill you?" Richard said.

"I don't want to die or become a vampire," Ernest whispered.

"You know Bree could do you, and you would actually enjoy it. No pain, but I think she would enjoy turning you even more. Think about it. Sex with a beauty then either –oblivion or awake into our life. She would also enjoy being your mistress."

"I just want to be my human self," Ernest pleaded.

"You know too much, but I appreciate your chronicle."

"Please," Ernest said, looking into his terrible eyes.

"Look, then. Write up the story as I have commanded. You can never go back anywhere to anyplace you described. Never, never, never, never!" His glowing eyes filled Ernest's brain which spun around until he passed out.

Next thing Ernest knew he was back in his home surrounded by his beloved paperbacks. Sandy was curled up on his stomach. Ralph was whining and begging for food. He raised himself from bed half conscious. He fell back, and half an hour later, he got out of bed.

Many times since that day he tried to find the two clubs: Flames of Love or the Bordello, but in the first case, he always wound up in front of the Bellagio's dancing waters, and in the latter, in front of the TI's Sirens set. No matter how hard he tried, he always ended up in exactly the same place. He couldn't even find Fangs, although there were references to it here and there.

Are there vampires or not? I just can't figure it out, Ernest thought. *Maybe the whole thing was just a nightmare, maybe not. Yet in my pocket, I found a book of matches with a sexy girl on the cover and printed in large block letters Bordello Club, and in smaller print, "It's legal in Nevada." No telephone number, no e-mail address, nothing more.*

THE VAMPIRE STATE

I. TRANSFORMATION

My obsession with vampires killed me, Ernest Frank realized later. Ernest kept searching for vampires until he found them. Unfortunately for him, he kept looking everywhere, trying to locate the night club where he first saw a vampire in action, and finally, despite a powerful spell that the vampire, Richard, placed on him to confuse his mind, he was able to find the Flames of Love. He walked in and acted like any other tourist making the rounds, played the innocent, but they knew. Richard knew that he had pierced the veil, broken through the spell.

Two burly bouncers grabbed him at the bar and pushed him towards the back entrance just as if he had been listed in the back book of excluded persons. He was not just thrown out on the street like some obnoxious drunk or a card counter—no, what happened was far worse than anything he could imagine.

Richard stared hard at him, with eyes that seemed to burn through his very soul. He stood unable to move, unable to scream, rooted to the ground by the vampire's power. Then the immortal spoke the awful words.

"We can't keep you away, so you must die, either to your world or the true death."

Ernest was in a daze, but he heard his own voice as if it was speaking from millions of miles away, distant and soft. "I don't want to die…"

"It won't hurt. Bree will take you gently. You'll just go to sleep and never wake up."

"No," Ernest's voice pleaded. "Let me live, please, please…"

"I can have her turn you then, but it might not work, and it will be painful."

"You never mentioned the pain…"

"You never asked, and why should I go into that much detail?"

"I want to live…"

"You will, but not as a human.

All his protests grew feeble, and Richard took him into a room and bid him wait a moment for his killer, so he sat down paralyzed, helpless, and afraid.

Bree was far more beautiful than he remembered from watching her while the vampire turned her. Her figure exuded sexuality, with beautiful hips, lovely breasts, but her eyes were arresting as she came into him.

"Don't be afraid," she said. "You and I will know a love like no mortal ever had, and afterward, you will be truly one of us." Bree smiled her lovely smile. She took him by the hand and led him to the bed. They sat down, and she began to kiss him. After a while, they came up for air, and she unbuttoned her top, unfastened her bra, and looked at him as he stripped off his shirt, trousers, and underwear.

"Kiss me, Ernie, everywhere!" she said. So he kissed each breast and then her lips again, then went down on her. His knees had stopped shaking, and astride her, he entered, driving, driving, and driving. In the very moment when he pushed into her, she kissed him on the lips, then her head darted to the side, and there was a sudden pain as she pierced his throat. In a second, the hurt faded, and then everything began to feel good. He exploded again with the intensity of the act. He felt dizzy, then excited, then dizzy. He was getting weaker, and finally, he was sleepy. The last thing he remembered was Bree slashed her wrist and extended it over his mouth, which she held open with her fingers.

"Drink," she said, "and live!" Then he drank and passed out.

When he woke up, his whole body began to shake. He was covered with sweat, and he headed to the toilet to throw up the entire contents of his stomach or so it seemed. The pain was terrible. Every part of his body was in flames. No sooner did he lie down than another attack worse than the first hit him. Then, the pain subsided just a little. Finally, he was heaving over the toilet, but nothing more came out. Then he collapsed on the bed, too weak to move, and passed out again. Still, he ached all over. Several times more, he woke to retch, and then he went to sleep.

Voices drifted into his mind.

"I think he will live," Richard said. "I wasn't sure the way the transformation hit him last night, but he is still with us. He needs blood urgently. Bring in the maid."

Maria Suarez was brown, beautiful, and delicious, and for the first time, fangs filled his mouth. The fangs brought a supremely weird feeling, and his stomach contracted with hunger pangs he had never known before.

"Don't take too much," cautioned Bree. "They still need her to clean rooms!"

Richard chuckled at that but stood close maybe so he could grab him if he fed too long. Bree encouraged the maid: "It won't hurt, Maria, and you'll heal fast. You'll have a job with us as long as you like."

The first sweet savor of blood was overwhelming as his fangs pierced her neck, and he was dizzy as he drew in the red stream. He was so hungry he could have drained the last drop from her there.

"That's enough, Ernie," Bree said. "Don't drink too much. It could make you sick again. Lie down and let your body adjust to its new food. From now on, you will always be a little hungry. It's a survival trait of our kind. You'll just have to get used to it."

"Bree will teach you to feed in ways that will not attract public attention," Richard said. "The first rule for every immortal is to never attract the eye of mortals or let them know we even exist. Those who didn't do this got a stake through the heart or were beheaded, if not by mortals, by their own kind. Silence is golden. Agreed?"

"Yeah, sure," he said, still mostly out of it. Then he fell asleep for a while. When he woke up, the lights were dim. He went over and peeked out of the window. The setting sun had painted the sky orange-red. Then he saw Bree standing as still as a statue in a corner of the room. It's a trick vampires have.

Ernest wrote about this later in his journal. "I'm sure you know this already because if you are reading this, you are an immortal. That is regrettable, in a way, because there is much we could teach mortals about life and death. In my earlier work, when I was still mortal, I was able to write about us, but what I could say was, well, limited by the need of our kind for secrecy. Now I can say more, but my mistress and her master still tell me to be careful what I write. Once, writing was my life, but now that I am dead to the world, it is only a hobby. Still, the *Immortal Chronicles* does give me a place to express my vision as does the *Everlasting Times*."

II. METAMORPHOSIS

Many mortals have joked about a city called Lost Wages, where visitors lose up to their last penny, but few of them know it as the true capital of the Vampire State. What, you say, isn't Carson City Capital of Nevada? Well, maybe once upon a time, but nominal and real things are often different. In the real world, Las Vegas rules.

It was Richard's Emily who found him. Sam Santiago was an up-and-coming prosecutor, but he liked the girls, and he visited Nights of Passion, a new cool club. Once he spotted Emily's fiery red hair, oval face, and lovely figure, he decided he just had to know this girl. Never mind that he was twenty years her senior, divorced, and with two children. Richard realized this was a golden opportunity for the immortal community. Emily, who worked at the club at night and at the House of Strange on weekends, needed to go carefully. Sam couldn't just be turned without consequences, not with two children in his house.

So Emily told him one weekend, "I really care for you and want to spend more time with you, but if I slept over, your children might not like it."

"John and Mary are old enough to know that their dad is a man who is looking for a woman in his life, a wife. They've accepted that my marriage to their mother is over, and I think they know I am looking for someone new."

"Right now, Sam, we need to build our relationship. We need time alone together. Maybe you could send them to camp for a week this summer?"

"Well, they like to spend vacation time with their mother sometime. Maybe I could set things up, so we could have a week or two all to ourselves."

"I'd like that," Emily replied with a smile, thinking that that would just be enough time to convert Sam and train him in our ways.

Emily told Ernest that during a white hot night of love, she bit Sam and completed his conversion. "It was incredible, the energy he had. He just kept going and going like the Energizer bunny, even while I was draining his life blood. And he gave me the most incredible orgasm I ever had. It blew me through the roof. He turned out to be a natural as a bloodsucker too. Richard had to yank him off the maid before he drained her entirely. By the time his kids came home, he had learned how to mask his identity completely. He told them he had developed a terrible allergy to sunlight. From then on, he started wearing long sleeves, hats, and dark glasses whenever he absolutely had to go out in the daytime."

Now Sam was famous because he had prosecuted the notorious Sally Ferrero. Sally, an incredible blonde beauty with curves in all the right places, had been first the mistress, then the wife of Big Richard Smith, part owner of the Golden Cornucopia Casino. Unfortunately, Big Richard became a heroin addict, and not the same generous lover he had been at the start, when the two of them were accustomed to party all day and night nonstop. So she fell in with Ronald Levy who had been a bouncer at one of the clubs where she worked. Big Richard died, but was it from a heroin overdose? If so, was it voluntary, or did Sally and Ronald do it? Sally claimed she loved Richard to the last and that she only partied with Ronald a couple of times when Big Richard was so zonked out from drugs, he didn't even wake up for days.

Sam went after the pair hammer and tongs, and he was backed a hundred percent by the powerful Smith clan who wanted to be sure that whatever happened, Sally didn't wind up in control of his estate, including his share of the Golden Cornucopia. Sam's triumph put the pair on death row and brought him the full and unconditional support of the Smith tribe.

The election of 2010 was one of the most exciting in the history of Nevada. Sam, now our man, was running for governor on the Conservative ticket, with multimillion-dollar support from the Smith family and half a dozen other big casino owners. Upon nomination, he declared, "Nevadans should know that if they elect me, there will be no new taxes. By cutting spending to the bone and trimming our bloated bureaucracy, we can help business restore the economy of our Nevada and bring back that prosperity which has long spurred growth in this land. End job-killing taxation Vote for me and vote for prosperity!"

Ozzie Stackford, the Liberal candidate, took a different stance. In a speech in Reno, on September 2, he laid out his position:

"In these difficult economic times, we do need to be careful of our spending. The truth is, however, we need to overhaul the entire tax system of Nevada. We cannot rely on property taxes and sales taxes based on discretionary spending alone. In hard times, the value of houses shrinks, and people cut back on their spending as much as they have to, but our public schools and universities still need money more than ever. They must prepare the leaders of tomorrow; our whole business climate depends on a well-educated work force.

"There is money available that we can get without increasing the average Nevadan's taxes. Gold mining companies are harvesting millions from the record price on gold and silver. Casinos too are making millions even in today's difficult economy. We should raise mining taxes and licensing fees for casinos. I need your votes to save Nevada and prepare it for a golden future."

Naturally, university professors, teachers' unions, retired people, and public interest groups wanted to support Stackford and the Liberals. Even the Latino community split, despite a gaffe Sam made when asked about a bill that might allow police to stop people and ask them about their citizenship status. No one will mistake my children for illegals, he said. (They were too white.) Naturally, that offended the browner Mexican Americans and maybe some Cubans.

Others such as the independents thought the whole election disgusting. Both parties hurled accusations of misconduct and corruption at one another. Liberals said that Sam had been a lawyer for Mafiosos before he was appointed prosecutor. Sam said that as attorney for the teachers' union, Ozzie had pocketed kickbacks from consultants. Both candidates accused the other of lobbying for fat cat corporations in the State assembly. This reached to the point where some were ready to vote libertarian or even to mark the "none of the above" box.

November 2 brought one of the greatest landslide votes in Nevada history. The casinos, mining companies, and wealthy business owners solidly backed Santiago. Never had they spent so much on an election. The voters responded as expected. The wealthy donors found their investment paid off for them very well.

III. THE FRUITS OF POWER

The inaugural ball was splendid indeed. It was right after a short ceremony, Nevada's first evening inauguration. Sam positively glowed as he stood in pride with his son and daughter. Emily attended, but not at the new governor's right hand as she would have liked. The wives of state assembly men, state senators, and judges dressed in glittering designer gowns mingled with those of casino owners, danced to the strains of the waltz, the fox trot, the tango, and for the younger set and the Latins, it was the salsa. The ballroom was festooned with garlands of laurel and decorated with palm branches emblematic of the Conservative victory. The victory was complete, but not quite as solid as Sam would have liked, for a fair number of Liberals were reelected to the assembly despite the bad economy. Emily enjoyed taking part in the fun, but there was disappointment too.

Sam, Richard, and Julia had made it all clear. Since Emily had worked as a hostess at the club and weekends at the Love Ranch, she could never marry Sam. She was not notorious, it was true, but somebody might remember her, and the consequences for the Governor might be disastrous, if the press got wind of it. Emily would be Sam's mistress forever, it was true, but the public must never know. She must exchange no e-mails that could be traced.

"Look," Richard said, "the woman we want for the new first lady is Clarissa Smith, the youngest sister of Big Richard. She is beautiful, and Sam will enjoy her, but best of all, it will make our alliance rock solid. Some mornings, she will wake up feeling really drained. After this, the new achievement, the new Satrap of Nevada will have to pay attention to me and give me important new responsibilities."

"What about me?" Emily asked.

"I would like you to become Clarissa's best friend and, should it ever become necessary, to turn her. Sam has not the skill for that yet. And you will be my eyes also. Of course, you will stop working for Strange at once. You can keep your job at the club for now."

"Darling, I will always love you and want to be with you as often and as long as I can. I do need to strengthen my relationship with the Smith family," Sam explained. "Through Clarissa, I can control her share of the Golden Cornucopia and use her family to advance our plans for immortal rule.

"Right now, I am facing incredible problems with the State budget, which must be balanced somehow. We are going to have to cut popular things like the public parks and, worst of all, education, not only the university system but even the public schools."

"How can you get the legislature to do that?" Julie asked. "The University supporters will yell about their role in bringing new businesses to Nevada. Parents want either to give their children a good education or at least to keep them out of their hair."

"Too many people think a university education is for everybody. That's a ridiculous notion. The University is for the sons and daughters of those who can pay and pay well. Of course, there are a few bright people who need scholarships or are so promising banks can make money financing their careers. As for the rest of Nevada youth, just look at their dismal graduation rates from high school. And this is not the high school I attended but a dumbed down version."

"Well, Sam, gaming doesn't require workers who are into rocket science," Richard observed, "and even high school dropouts can work as valet car parkers."

"We need to get the growth engine started again and that requires low taxes, and one other thing—water. Right now, Las Vegas is at the limit of the water it can take from the Colorado. We need water from north, but that will require millions of dollars to construct a giant pipeline. The Water Authority is at work on it as we speak."

"Won't the Indians, ranchers, and townspeople in the north object?"

"Sure, they will." Sam smiled. "But the Liberals have given us just the tools we need. The US Supreme Court has ruled one man one vote, and the votes are in Las Vegas, not in on the Indian reservations, northern ranches, Carson City, or Reno. I mean to suck the north dry. When we get through, Las Vegas will have all the water it needs, and the north will become a wasteland like the Sahara. Who cares about a few ranchers and Indians anyway?"

The grand ball continued on late into the night, but just after the clock struck nine, Richard and Emily approached Clarissa who was talking to Sam.

"Sam and Clarissa Smith, I'd like you to meet Emily. You know, Sam, she's your number one fan. I think you might know her from the club Nights."

"I never forget a face, especially as pretty a one as yours, young lady. Yes, I think I even danced with you once. It's a pleasure to see you here."

Then he turned back to Clarissa and continued, "As you know, Clarissa, I'm no longer married, and I need someone to act as official hostess, at the mansion for parties and the like. I would love it if you would consider taking up the post."

"Well, I'd have to think about it," she said with a lovely smile. Sam knew at once from her pleased expression he had hit the mark dead on.

IV. Making It Happen

The Nevada legislature was in turmoil. The Liberals declared the Governor's budget dead on arrival. Assemblyman Richard Hermann, spokesman for the Liberal party, declared that cutting funds for education was "simply not acceptable."

"Nevada already has the lowest per pupil spending in the nation," he declared. "There is simply no way we can continue to improve education without more money for computers and software, teachers, textbooks, everything."

The Liberal Party members rose as one body to give the speech their enthusiastic applause.

Roland Smith, a Conservative from Las Vegas, rose to defend the Governor. "This budget is the best we can do. I agree that education is important, but tell me where we can get the money without raising taxes. With our economy, the way it is that is simply impossible."

Meanwhile, Richard Rich, a black Liberal from North Las Vegas, submitted a bill for a raise in the casino tax, the same one he submitted every session, and as usual, it never reached the floor. Although he always faced well-funded opponents every election, even in the primary, and from his own party, he always managed to be reelected. He was the gad-fly of the casino empires.

Meanwhile, the Nevada-elected Supreme Court judges, always benefiting from the largesse of the casino lords, declared that the teachers' union initiative petition for a business tax to support education invalid because in contained language that was "obscure and lacking in clarity." Surprise (not)! Bite the hand that feeds them, never!

In short, everything going on in the legislature and State was totally chaotic and entirely normal.

In his third news conference after the election, Sam made an announcement: "You will observe that in this year's budget, we have zero funded the State park system. We are closing all the parks effective next Monday due to a lack of money to keep them open. We do have a partial solution worked out for the closure. Mr. Richard York and a group of leading entertainment entrepreneurs have agreed to form a corporation, Nevada Recreation, to reopen the most popular public parks as a for profit operation and at no cost to the public. Nevada will continue to own its parks. They will reopen to its people. Users will pay to enjoy them and all at no cost to our government. The contract will run two years with the possibility of a renewal. I'm hoping that our fiscal reforms will allow us to reestablish a pared-down system of parks when the economy improves."

Richard smiled when he heard this, and he had already made a deal with Strange to open new houses in some of the more remote parks. That way, visitors could enjoy beauty in forms never intended by those who funded Nevada's parks. It might even be possible to reopen some of the most famous and storied brothels in Nevada's ghost towns, using real whores dressed in costumes from the State's past. Some of them, in fact, might have once worked there!

One of the biggest fights was over cuts to the Nevada University, especially to its southern campus, in Las Vegas. President Maxim Minimus pointed out that Nevada needed to build up its research facilities and become more than a school of hotel administration, a basketball power, and a party school. The University had its School for Desert Studies, a school that would be badly hurt from the 30 percent cut in funding Sam was demanding.

"Cuts of the magnitude will make our University only another cow-country college. No one will take us seriously or provide us with research grants or contracts for important investigations. We won't be able to recruit first-rate faculty or staff, and serious students will look elsewhere for an education."

Meanwhile, Sam scoured the State for money. He demanded that unspent appropriations be returned to the State's coffers by the localities and special agencies that had received them. Counties, cities, and agencies scrambled to bring suit in court to stop Sam from draining the last of their already depleted funds. Then came a disappointment. The Supreme Court declared that the funds could only be spent for the original purposes of the grants. Liberals everywhere breathed a sigh of relief.

The marriage of Sam and Clarissa was the social event of the season. Sam positively glowed while Clarissa was smiling but just a little pale in her white gown. She pushed aside her veil and accepted the kiss from her groom. Sam's courtship had had an easy and natural progression. From dinner meetings to discuss her role as official hostess to movie dates and partying at Nights to weekend cruises at Lake Mead and getaways at his cabin in the woods.

Sam had offered the ring on bended knee, just as in the romantic movies that delighted Clarissa so. She accepted him with joy, for he was truly a catch, handsome, wealthy, and powerful. In short, he was everything she had ever desired in a man. Theirs would be a political alliance she knew, but a lot more as well. Sam, on the other hand, rejoiced in his trophy wife and enjoyed serving a powerful mistress as well.

Sam was the idol of Conservatives everywhere. A family man, a fiscal conservative, and upholder of traditional values. A Latin who opposed illegal immigration, he could well be a choice for the next US senatorial race or even a presidential candidate. The rare beauty of his wife made them truly a gilded couple, a hope for the future of their party.

At this point, Sam swerved slightly. Thus far, he had held rigidly to his no new taxes theme. Now he said that he might not consider renewing of expiring taxes a new tax. Certain taxes were supposed to expire; Sam decided to extend them.

"It's this way," he explained. "I was counting on some of the money left over from previous appropriations to complete my budget. Without that money, I have to find funds from some other place. No, I don't like taxation, especially now, but we have to have money from somewhere."

When he heard about Sam's changing stance Stackford, whom he had beaten in the election and many Liberals were very pleased. Ozzie put it this way. "I had almost given up on our Governor who seemed to have no regard for Nevada at all. Now I see that lurking behind his partisan, no-taxes façade, there might be a little statesman after all."

Despite this, the Clark County School District had to shorten the school year by forty days after the arbitrators ruled it couldn't implement its plan to slash teacher pay by half. As a result, the district had to double class size and tell five hundred new teachers who had been scheduled to start in September, there were simply no jobs.

The University system closed one college and consolidated two so that the first two years of a four-year school were dropped, and students redirected to complete their initial studies in a community college. The Community College learned that it would not become a four-year school, after all. The former four-year school now offered just the final two years and a bachelor's degree in general studies. The University reluctantly closed a number of degree programs including one in desert studies.

V. AT THE VERTEX

Richard York, the vampire who had Ernest turned, also basked in the glory of the Conservative victory.

"Great news," he told Ernest one morning. "The Las Vegas Satrap has named me to the vampire Commission on The General Peace and Order, and he has submitted my name to the King for his honors list. 'Lord of the Vegas Night', it might be, or perhaps 'Lord of the Mountain Shadows' or even 'Eternal Guardian of the Southern Realm.' How do they sound?"

"Well," Ernest said after a moment's thought, "I think the last title sounds best. The others sound like something a Las Vegas club owner or real estate developer might dream up. What effect will all this have for you in practical terms?"

"Not only am I going to be in charge of exploiting the park system, but I will be running at least three of the hottest night spots in town. All my girls are very excited."

"You mean that now you will be running Flames, Nights, and the Bordello Club?"

"Weren't you on the outs with the new administration after the King killed the old Satrap?"

"All of that is long forgotten mostly because Sam supports me. He understands the power of us vampires and knows that in a pinch, we could be very useful to his administration and, long term, to his political future."

"Richard, what are you going to do with the State parks?"

"Well, we will hire daytime staff to charge $25 apiece for all individuals who want to camp out overnight in the parks. Weekly fees will be $150. Simple daytime visitors will have to pay $15 each. Some of us will do special night time programs, taking advantage of our superior hearing and sense of smell. Vampires should make really good guides for nighttime walks, and of course, some of the visitors will be contributing something extra for their experiences. Some of the more remote parks I will just close or turn over to Strange to establish houses there. He will pay us 25 percent of his profits. Half of that will go the Las Vegas Satrap. The rest of the revenue goes to our corporation, with a nice kickback for Sam, of course."

"Wouldn't that be illegal?" Ernest asked.

"The law seldom stops Nevada politicians from getting what they want. Anyway, Nevada is now the Vampire State. It's the beginning of a whole new era, in many ways like the old but with a metamorphosis, a system-wide transformation that will change everything into our image with the passage of time."

"I suggest, as your counselor," Ernest said, "that you play it straight. Cash is too easy to trace, and you can offer Sam benefits that will be…untraceable but still very…pleasing." *Some vampires*, he reflected, *think they're above the law*, but he kept his mouth shut. *Wasn't I one of them?* he thought.

VI. THE WHEEL TURNS

Nevadans were all shocked when we got word an appellate court had overturned the murder conviction of Sally Ferrero and her lover. The story on the evening news was all but unbelievable. Roger Stackford, younger brother of Ozzie, an attorney for Sally and her boyfriend declared, "We knew there was evidence that the prosecutor concealed from us at discovery. A witness had reported that Big Richard purchased a large amount of heroin the night before he died. The prosecutor told him that if he wouldn't say anything, he wouldn't bring charges of selling drugs, charges that could land him in prison for forty years. Unfortunately for the prosecution, there was another witness, a small-time user who was there too. He didn't have the same fears, and he came to us after the trial.

"The court ruled the trial a substantial miscarriage of justice and annulled the verdict. Even the prosecutors couldn't make up their minds as to the real cause of Big Richard's death. Did Ronald sit on the chest of the drugged man, or did the two of them force him to take drugs. If he went willingly to buy drugs, the court ruled it was unlikely that they simply forced him to take an overdose. Santiago's concealment of the evidence was enough all by itself, to justify reversal of the conviction."

"What are we going to do?" Richard asked. "This could destroy all our plans. It will undermine Sam's administration also cause real problems for the Smith family. Sally could wind up controlling a quarter of the Golden Cornucopia. Not to mention millions of dollars, besides. All that gold, he hoarded. Big Richard was too generous in his will. He should have cancelled it when he tired of that whore, but he didn't."

"Take it easy," Ernest advised. "Panic won't help. Think. What will the Liberals do about this? How will they attack the Governor? They don't have the votes for impeachment. Their best shot will be federal intervention. What tactics will federal prosecutors use? What court would hear the case? Also, I think the courts will be reluctant to restore Sally's share of the estate. The Smiths can claim with some justice that Big Richard was under the influence of drugs when he changed his will in Sally's favor. That should help them keep the property settlement more or less the way it worked out after Sally's conviction. They might have to repay her for some of the small bequests. Also, they can string the case out in court for years if need be, but Sally has no money."

VII. DISASTER STRIKES

Sam was happy when Ernest saw him despite the fact that Sally's conviction had been overturned. He was whistling as he walked over to us after his visit with Emily. Sam looked quite distinguished as he had already begun to brush in gray into his sideburns to counteract the effects of vampiric restoration. Later, more and heavier make up would be needed, and eventually, he would have to "die" in a tragic accident and start life somewhere else. Just now, he seemed unaware of just how serious his problems were becoming.

"Good news! Clarissa is expecting," he said, as he came up to Richard and myself. "I'm going to be a father again."

"Don't you remember that we warned you about that?" Richard remarked. "The child will be half-vampire and that will make the pregnancy very difficult for Clarissa, maybe even fatal. The best way to save her will be to turn her, but then, she will have to know."

"Oh no! I have no idea whether she will be able to accept that and everything that goes with it." His face fell.

"What are we going to do about the fact that the court freed Sally?" Richard asked. "The court cited the fact you concealed that Big Richard himself bought the dope that killed him. Your prosecutors covered that up, and your enemies will be all over you about it."

Sam's expression hardened. "I know how to deal with them. They can't prove that I personally knew anything about the witness. There were many lawyers in my office and many cases on my desk."

"True enough," Ernest said, "but you took great pride that you *personally* handled the Ferrero case, a claim which could now bite you in the butt."

"Santiago should resign," Ozzie Stackford declared at a press conference, in a story picked up on the front page of the *Las Vegas Sun*. "His bogus prosecution, no, persecution of Sally Ferrero at the behest of the powerful Smith family was wrong from the start and his concealing of evidence was a criminal offense. If he doesn't resign, he should be impeached."

A week later, Hermann introduced a bill of impeachment into the Nevada Assembly with a fiery speech: "We need to get rid of the worst Governor that the State of Nevada has ever had, and all his flunkies with him. Impeaching him for his undoubted crime will clean up this State and get us back on track to a government of which we may be proud."

After a series of hearings where comments followed more or less party-line opinions, the Governor testified he had no personal knowledge of his office's concealment of evidence that Big Richard had purchased heroin himself just before he died.

"We were working on the theory that either Sally or her lover bought it, knowing of the man's weakness, and deliberately made up a fatal dose for him. It does appear we were mistaken, but there is little question that Sally exploited him to the utmost. Just maybe, just possibly, Big Richard's death was accidental. Personally, I have my doubts, but considering the new evidence, the court was correct to reverse Sally's conviction. There is room for reasonable doubt."

Little new evidence came to light during the hearings, and in due course, Hermann and the Liberals brought the bill to the floor, where it failed on a straight party line vote. Sam had dodged the bullet.

Meanwhile, after the usual wrangling, the Nevada legislature approved a budget and wrapped up its biennial session and adjourned *sine die*. Sam and the Conservatives could breathe a sigh of relief.

Clarissa's pregnancy was indeed proving problematic. Sam advised her to see an immortal doctor, who had experience with these situations. She did not know, of course, that he was anything more than a specialist with experience in handling difficult pregnancies.

"In such cases," Dr. Lauren Fabian told Sam, "the outcome often depends on whether the baby is more vampire or more human. The mother has a much greater chance of surviving if the child is human than if a vampire. Vampire babies require different nutriments to do well. I will give her some supplements, but my advice would be to tell her the truth and turn her before the sixth month. Especially, if the baby, as it appears, will be a vampire child."

When the seventh month came, it was already almost too late. Clarissa already looked like a blimp while her eyes were sunken and her arms and legs rail thin. Sam, Richard, and Emily realized they had to take emergency action. Actually, Emily was not so concerned that Clarissa would die as that Sam, who had come to love his wife, would hate her if she couldn't help save both the mother and child.

"Look," she said to Sam as they had gathered outside her bedroom. "It has to be now if you want to save her. Your son may not make it, and if he does, he is going to have problems. Growing up half vampire is terrible.

"Anything, I'll do anything, but save her. Save the child if you can. You must save her."

"Then do this. Kiss her one last time as a human, then drink her blood. Next, Dr. Fabian will administer a transfusion of your blood that you gave before. It will keep her and the baby from dying. The change in blood will provide the child what he needs, and now, it should save Clarissa too."

Trembling, Sam bent over his wife to kiss her, then suddenly plunged his fangs in to drain her. At the very moment, her heart trembled from the change in pressure, the transfusion kicked in flooding her with vampire blood.

Clarissa went pale, then flushed. She shook all over and began to perspire. She tried to get up. They held her. She retched up the contents of her stomach into a basin. She had to be held down, and her shrieks were heartrending.

"What have you *done* to me!" she shouted. "What have you done to me! What have you…"

She passed out. She struggled continually nonetheless, thrashing to and fro on her bed. Finally the struggling slowed, and she muttered a few words. "I thought…I thought you loved me." Then she stopped and lay still.

Clarissa awoke, her eyes glowing bright red, her new fangs descending for the first time as she looked wildly around the room. She rose violently from her bed and charged the nurse who had just come in. She was ravenous. She was thirsting to feed two vampires, not one. In a flash, she was on the woman who screamed just once before the fangs tore into her jugular vein. Then there was a little gurgle, and the victim rolled her eyes before she passed out.

"Get her off that woman now, or she'll kill her," Dr. Fabian screamed, while Richard, Emily and Ernest pulled her off with all their might.

"Bring in Maria," Richard yelled because the woman Clarissa had attacked was a not the food source he had arranged to bring in at all. A second maid was also waiting, but they sent the second woman home because Clarissa was already slated from drinking from the nurse beforehand.

After feeding from Maria, Clarissa settled down, and they were able to get her back on to the bed to digest her first regular meal as a vampire. She quickly went back to sleep.

The next few months were a wonder to behold. Ernest was able to see the something no mortal had ever seen, the birth of a vampire child. It was, however, not unlike the birth of a normal human.

What was really different was that vampire mothers all have pink milk. Not only do their breasts secrete milk, they also combine it with their own blood so as to provide a nutritious mixture the baby thrives on.

Clarissa loved her baby but was much less understanding about Sam. Nor was she entirely happy to be spending eternity or least thousands of years as a bloodsucker.

"Why did you lie to me, Sam? Why didn't you tell me who you really were? I loved you, and you already belonged to Emily. Now I'm a freak. I didn't tell you to do that to me or want you to do it. It's disgusting."

"Look, we had to do it, or you would have died," Sam replied. "We didn't have time to talk you through it. Not only that, but our new son would have perished too."

"Couldn't you have told me before I got pregnant? I was so happy to be giving you a new son, our new son. And you were cheating all along."

"For God's sake, Clarissa. I met Emily long before I met you. She herself told me vampire relations can't be exclusive in a human sense, or they would have all starved to death centuries ago. She gave her blessing to our marriage, became your friend, helped save you and our baby's life."

"I am going to need some time, some space to decide what to do Sam. I just wish I had known you were a vampire before I got pregnant. Why didn't you tell me before I married you?"

"For God's sake. It's a capital offense to tell any human about us. Secrecy is a prime vampire directive."

"I just don't know, Sam. I just don't know. But I'll figure it out. I will, and then, I'll know what to do."

All the newspapers picked up on it when Nevada's first lady moved out of the mansion to a small house of her own, taking her new baby with her. Sam still visited her often hoping that reconciliation would come soon.

VIII. THE FALL

It was autumn in Nevada. School children were returning to their classes. True, the leaves were still green on the trees, but they would stay that way until late November. The summer heat had just begun to ease a little. Some days didn't reach a hundred degrees. Not a bad time for most Nevadans, but for Sam and Richard, it became a terrible time.

Mid-September, the headlines of the *Las Vegas Review-Journal* announced the news to the world. "Federal indictment brought against Governor Sam Santiago. Witness reports that he called his office from Lake Tahoe, California, to ask if they had persuaded drug dealer to remain silent about Big Richard's drug buy. Governor arrested at mansion, released on twenty million dollars bail."

Two days later, the Governor committed suicide, jumping from the Colorado bridge, striking the rocky soil below with such force that a mesquite branch pierced his heart. Clarissa, Richard, and Emily mysteriously disappeared, as did John Strange. No one would ever see them again. It was rumored that they were fugitives from justice. Ernest knew better. Somewhere in the vast Nevada desert, they were staked to the ground, hand and foot with silver chains. When dawn came and the flaming sun rose over the horizon, they would begin to die, but it wouldn't be fast. There would be the agony of burning flesh, horrible screams, and finally, after several hours they would expire. Sometimes, the cruelest executioners even left humans with them to squirt water into their mouths to prolong the agony for a few hours more. Then they were toast, toast burnt black.

The night, after the Governor's suicide, two huge men appeared at Ernest's door, forced their way into his house, and seized him with their hands pushing him back into a chair.

One said, "You are really lucky, Ernie. You're nobody, and you didn't choose to become a vampire. You were forced into the change. You're just not worth killing."

The other said, "Just don't attract the attention of the mortal world to vampires. Don't make a spectacle of yourself or any of the rest of us, and you will keep on living."

IX. THE WINTER OF OUR DISCONTENT

"It seems then," Ernest mused, "that I will not perish soon. I have the skills now a vampire needs to prolong his existence. Yet I wonder about things. Did Clarissa reconcile with Sam before her death? Were her executioners relentless, or did they show mercy because she had not chosen to be a vampire? What happened to the child she bore Sam?

"Somewhere from my distant university days, words popped into my brain, something from Latin 111. *O fortuna, velut luna, statu veriablis.* Fortune is always changing like the moon. Her wheel is in ceaseless motion, transforming human, and yes, vampiric affairs. *Rex sedet in vertice, caveat ruinam, nam sub axe legimus, Hecubam reginam.* Even a vampire king, sitting at the summit of power is subject to fate, and beneath the axis of fortune's wheel lies only death and oblivion.

"Someday, would I see Christ on the final day, or be cast into hell for all eternity? I did not choose to become a vampire. I was forced into it. As was the luckless Clarissa. No, that is not true. Richard offered me death, if I wished, but I chose life, or did I? All I can do now is do the best I can with others. I must feed, but I need not kill. Perhaps, just maybe, if I throw myself on God's mercy, he will understand why I made a wrong choice. I should have trusted in Jesus and perished rather than following my natural instinct and trying to keep on living. Can he forgive me for that? One day, I will know."

HAROLD HALBMANN

I. A VAMPIRE CHILDHOOD

It was several months before Julia Strange could bring herself to tell Ernest how worried she was that day. Julia had been Richard York's first turn and had married John Strange. She was happy at the time. All seemed to be going well until the federal authorities indicted Sam Santiago, the then Governor of Nevada, for previous illegal conduct as a prosecutor.

Julia, a tall, gorgeous brunette, had been a showgirl when Richard transformed her, had long suffered so much remorse about becoming a vampire that her sire had feared he might have to destroy her, but had finally accepted her new life, settled into work in Strange's brothel, and married him. Now, she was there as the madam.

Summoned by special emissaries of the King of all Vampires, Palaeologos X, He Whose Name No Mortal May Hear, John had left one morning for a meeting with Sam, Clarissa, Richard, Emily, and maybe others to discuss how to deal with the indictment crisis. None of them was ever seen again except for Sam, who was found on the rocks below the Colorado Bridge with a sage brush branch through the heart.

Julia had been startled the evening of the meeting by a call from Judy Clayborne, Clarissa's babysitter, that she had called several numbers on the emergency contact list before hers, including Sam's, Richard's, and Emily's, all to no avail. She wanted to give the baby to someone and be paid for her time, including four extra hours.

Julia knew Clarissa would never willingly abandon her child and promised to come over and take charge. Something was really badly wrong she knew as she hurried to her truck and went to pick up the boy. Next day, when they found Sam, she knew that Clarissa must be dead too. And this happened just when Sam had begun to make some headway to patching up his marriage with her. Alas, all that was only history now.

Thus Julia became the guardian and surrogate mother of Harold Halbmann. Harold was really Harold Santiago or Smith perhaps, but his new mom knew that she would have to conceal his identity from He Whose Name No Mortal May Speak. The King might fear the child or at least kill him to keep his identity as a vampire secret.

Now raising a vampire child was not easy, Julia had heard. Even if you discarded the problem of providing an appropriate diet, there were issues of establishing self-control, dealing with strength and temperament. Vampire kids can be demanding and are so strong that a tantrum can turn all the furniture in a room to kindling and leave holes punched right through sheet rock walls to boot. It was best to raise them in stone-walled castles with heavy medieval furnishings, but even those are broken sometimes. Not even an adult vampire can really control child vampires by force. Blows only awaken their fury. Their little eyes would just go red with rage as they screamed and struck out in all directions, all but oblivious of any pain. Vampires require rewards for behavior parents wish to encourage; otherwise, their guardians can deny them some favorite activity to discourage misbehavior. Also, you couldn't safely raise them with human children either, as their rough play could easily break bones. They can heal easily, but humans cannot.

Then too, Julia had mused, just how would Harold develop, considering his mother's difficult pregnancy? He hadn't had proper nutrition until they turned his mother in the seventh month. Julia knew she just couldn't hand Harold over to Child Protective Services. What could they do with a vampire? Doing that would certainly doom poor Harold and maybe a couple of the workers over there too. It would be a violation of basic vampire directives to keep themselves from human awareness.

Julia just had to save him, and she had a cottage apart from the brothel. It was hers alone with John gone and with a maid too. She was relieved when, after running a temperature, wailing, and thrashing about, Harold's first teeth appeared. Once their children's fangs descended, vampire mothers weaned their children for obvious reasons.

As a two-year-old, Harold was already a handful. He took his toys apart for some reason Julia never understood. He liked to take the wheels off toy cars and trains, and he delighted in disassembling clocks. Alas, he could never put them back together. Curious about everything, constantly getting into things, he was in perpetual motion.

Harold had pronunciation and attention problems, and Julia took him to the best vampire doctors, only to discover he had attention deficit disorder, and later, after she tried to teach him to read, it was discovered that he had dyslexia, a disorder which causes its victims to see some letters reversed or differently from the way people normally see them. Fortunately, the brothel was profitable, and Julia had the money to send him to therapists. Gradually, he began to improve, first in pronunciation, later in reading. Ernest helped her with some tutoring efforts in reading, languages, and history.

Harold was a lonely child as there were few vampire children in Las Vegas, and Julia did not have the liberty to travel much. He loved video games and spent hours on his Play Station and Xbox. Mortal Combat was a favorite. He was so intent on finding the secret codes to reach more advanced levels of performance that he forced himself to overcome dyslexia. Yet he did overcome the problem or was able to compensate for it enough to read, not with ease or enjoyment, but for information. He clung to his Aunt Julia too much, maybe. He loved her as the mother he never knew.

The biggest problem was training Harold in the necessary self-restraint, so he could pass as human and finally attend middle and high school. He had to curb his hunger and not feed openly on a luckless student. He learned to keep from attacking someone who had a bloody nose or a bleeding cut. He had to turn away and keep his mouth closed so no one would see his fangs descend. He could pretend to be squeamish at the sight of blood lest someone see the flash of his eyes.

"Look," Ernest told him, "when you feed, after making very sure you are alone, that no one can come upon you accidentally, you need to look into the person's eyes, concentrate your mind with the message: 'Submit and know pleasure.' Then pierce the neck with a rapid stroke and draw a few ounces of blood. Count to yourself as you draw it—10, 9, 8, 7, 6, 5, 4, 3, 2, 1, 0—then step back. Never count from higher than 30, unless you mean to kill."

"Must I only bite women?"

"No, but feeding from the opposite sex is more fun and more normal. The embrace is linked to sexuality, so women are more apt to submit easily." Ernest spent more explaining how to date women, get them apart, and then afterward, kiss the wounds and heal with your saliva. "Most women will find you very hot," Ernest said. "After all, you are a vampire. Don't be like me when I was human. Ask an attractive girl to go out to the movies for dinner. She will surrender to your charms. Feed, during the date, heal the wound, then plant the suggestion that she had a wonderful evening with you. She will want to see you again."

Next, Ernest conducted a practical exercise with one of the maids. They were used to feeding Harold, but Ernest told them to do their best to remember all that happened when he did. Then he had Harold bite her, using his new feed-and-be-forgotten techniques. Afterward, Ernest ask her what happened. "When is he going to feed from me?" she asked afterwards. So Ernest knew he was making progress.

Then he cautioned him about what he couldn't do. He had to learn he must not throw a football farther than anyone else or run faster or smash a bully's skull. Being an indifferent athlete—a run-of-the-mill, lazy student—all that was life. Being a super athlete or hero was death.

One day, when Ernest criticized him sharply for displaying rage, Harold struck him in the arm and broke it, and he swerved off the road. Fortunately, there was no other traffic. He hit the curb, and the airbag inflated. Naturally, he healed within minutes, but he pointed out to Harold that you can't behave that way around humans who don't mend so rapidly.

Harold became multilingual, and besides English, he could talk Spanish or Latin with older vampires. Latin may be a dead language, but some vampires from Roman times still speak it. Reading foreign languages was another problem, and he would always have problems learning to read texts of any kind. He would always struggle with English spelling.

On his sixteenth birthday, Julia called him aside for a very special talk.

"Harold, I have not told you all this. You must remember and never forget this. You are the rarest of all of us, a natural-born vampire, something that normally happens only once in a century. I was only turned into a vampire. You were born that way. You are superior to all men and will be more powerful than most vampires one day very soon. You are the son of a man who once governed the State of Nevada and also of Clarissa Smith. That makes you special as a person and as an immortal. You will have two special and enduring tasks. First, from the shadows, unobserved and unnoticed by men, you will stand over the house of Smith as a guardian. They must never know it. Generations will come and go, and you will see everything. In time, you will read their minds, be able to anticipate human actions. You will destroy whoever seeks to do them great harm, and frustrate those who try to hurt them in smaller ways. You will be a true and just defender of your house."

"What is my second job? Aunt Julie. You said there were two tasks?"

"The second one you must do three to five centuries from now, when your power reaches its maximum. Please don't hurry. Build your strength, for you will need every ounce. On that day, you must go before Him Whose Name No Mortal May Speak, and then you must say it. "Palaeologos," tell him then, "I challenge you to single combat, to the death, for the murder of my mother and father, for countless others and all your crimes and injustice." Look straight into his eyes with yours and let him see there the fire of your anger. Then strike with all your might. You must be the survivor. Cut off his head and throw it into the flames. If he does not fight you to the death, stake him out in the sun as he did with your parents. He tricked them into their deaths as he did with my husband and poor Emily too. Then make it all worthwhile, reign as the most just, kindest vampire king who ever ruled. Until then, tell no one, vampire or human, who you are or what your mission is, and above all, learn to hide your thoughts even from the masters. Only trust Delia, and only talk of this to her when the time for action draws near. Don't even think about this in the presence of another vampire. If he has even the slightest notion of this, the vampire King will lay a trap and destroy you before you can challenge him. Once you challenge, he will have to do his own dirty work, but only one of you will walk away. Let it be you."

Then Julia changed her tone. "You are growing up. Enjoy being a kid. Study. Go to the university and take the degree that appeals to you. Find a special woman, vampire or human, and turn her if need be, raise your own children. Clarissa, your mother, feared immortality. You must embrace it. Live a rich life first, then seize the crown—your destiny."

Julia explained all this to Ernest two centuries later, after events I will relate, when these details could no longer endanger Harold. One of the good things about writing vampire history is that you have a chance to be both a contemporary witness and really view things in perspective. In other words, you're around long enough to find out how they work out. Yet some of it, Ernest might have guessed, and there was certainly similar danger from the vampire King. He was unconcerned about Sam's human children who could pose no danger to his power. He sought to locate his vampire child; fortunately, Julia had taken Clarissa's address book, and the King's prowling agents were unable to discover who was babysitting the child, even though they broke into Clarissa's house to search it and later pretended to be policemen when they interviewed the neighbors. Fortunately, the King's interest in the baby came as an afterthought. Vampire policies of secrecy militated against trying King Herod's attempted solution.

II. HAROLD'S EDUCATION

Harold was a fairly popular student at St. Peter's High School. He pestered his aunt to buy an old red Firebird (against Ernest's advice) and got a traffic ticket on the day he purchased and first drove it. Several more speeding tickets followed the following year. Harold studied hard, partied hard, avoided participating in sports, and shunned the limelight. Dark-haired, brown-eyed, square-jawed, he was popular with the girls and dated a good many. Then he courted a pretty Bulgarian immigrant for a while and took her to the prom. Her mother soon moved away from Las Vegas, and although the kids exchanged e-mails awhile, she soon found a guy at her new school and lost interest in Harold.

Harold did well in mathematics but was not so successful in subjects that required extensive reading. So Julia would read his textbooks aloud to him, or she would ask Ernest. Harold finished high school with a bare three-point average.

When he entered Nevada University, Harold chose business administration as his major. Given his abilities and his limitations, this was natural, but there is also a strong tradition of vampires who amass vast wealth in business over the centuries.

Naturally, the school also required liberal arts courses, so Harold asked Ernest to read for him again.

"I hate history. Why study it? I mean, it's all past anyway, and I'm interested in the future. What is the use of it?" he complained after starting on US history to 1865.

"Well, if you want to know why things are the way they are, history provides most of the explanations," Ernest advised. "For example, why do Mexicans speak Spanish, Brazilians, speak Portuguese, and some Canadians, French, and people here in the United States speak English? History gives us the answers, as you are about to learn. Also, because of who you are, you will actually get to talk to some of the people who were there back in the day. For purposes of your course, however, you had better cite written texts."

One day, as Ernest was working with Harold, a beautiful young woman came in. Ernest said, "I want you to meet Delia, one from our community here in Las Vegas. Delia, this is Harold Halbmann."

"It's good to meet you," she said. "I know about you and want to help you."

"Delia from Delos will introduce you to at least some of those who were eye witnesses to history," Ernest said, "although vampires were not there on every occasion." Ernest turned to Delia, "Delia, could you tell Harold something remarkable that you remember from your girlhood?"

Delia nodded and said, "When I was just a young girl, I was witness to the swift Leonidas of Rhodes first victory at the Olympics. After that, he went on to triumph in races at four succeeding games, unheard of at the time, but I was married by then, and we married ladies were not allowed to watch in those days."

"When was that, in 1936?" Harold asked.

"No, Harold, many centuries earlier," she said with a smile.

"In those days, they measured time by counting the Olympics, but in modern time, Leonidas first won his victor's crown in 164 BC," Ernest noted. "Since then, Delia has seen many centuries yet retains her beauty. You may ask about events in ancient Greece, Rome, and Byzantine times as she spent most of her time in the east."

Besides Harold's academic studies, Julia rightly insisted he work on his combat skills, both with weapons and without. Vampires are stronger and faster than humans, but they still need to learn how to put these abilities into action. Another power, that of reading minds comes more slowly and seems to begin with an ability to tell from a person's body language what he or she is about to do, then deepens into almost full power to read human minds and even those of newer vampires. Immortals have far better vision and hearing than most humans and their noses can detect subtle differences in odors. They learn the arts of stealthy movement easily, freezing themselves absolutely immobile against backdrops (never against the skyline) and thus make themselves all but invisible in the dusk or darkness.

Chuck Phillips taught Harold, although unarmed, how to deal with enemies with pistols, rifles, and shotguns. When they stood only a short distance away, the trick was to watch when their trigger finger started its movement, which means the shooter's whole attention was on hitting his target, and in that fraction of a second, Harold was to go from stand still to incredible speed, dropping and lunging forward at high velocity to strike his opponent's lower body even before he could fire. The overconfidence of an armed man facing someone without weapons was an important factor, but the key to remaining uninjured was to move at exactly that moment when the shooter shifted from scanning his overall target to firing. While immortals could recover from most wounds except losing their entire heads or hearts, the wounds would be painful, and depending on the loss of tissue, healing was energy consuming.

Phillips also encouraged Harold to learn to use the sword, one of the traditional weapons vampires favor.

"Remember," he reminded Harold, "a thrust exactly through the heart will kill any vampire as well as decapitation, so we immortals favor both thrusting and cutting weapons. The wisest understand that thrusting weapons are faster since they do not require the swordsman to draw back his weapon. Vampires use the small sword or the rapier. They also know the saber and broadsword. Japanese immortals prefer the katana.

"The basic stance for both the small sword and saber are similar. Form a ninety-degree angle with your feet, the right foot pointing toward your opponent, then take a short step forward, and bend your knees slightly. Your left leg is a spring that will drive you forward. First, extend your sword arm forward and then step forward as far as you can reach until your point touches the target. This is called the lunge or development. Try it a few times first without a weapon.

After Harold tried it several times at only human speed, Phillips handed him a sword and told him, "Now strike the figure on the wall at your normal speed."

Harold did as told, and he planted his point directly upon the figure of a heart on the wall, so fast that mortals would have seen only a blur. When immortals fence, mortal bystanders complain it is boring because they move so quick all they can see is a blur and hear, of course, the clash of steel on steel when someone parries. Immortals can follow the action much better.

"Very good!" Phillips said. "Very good! I believe you have the makings of a first-class swordsman."

Harold proved a good pupil, and soon, he knew all the eight traditional guards and could execute lightening attacks with the dueling sword and the saber. He spent countless hours perfecting his skills, his speed, and developing the stamina needed by the immortal swordsman.

Another traditional weapon favored by the vampires was the crossbow, which can be very deadly in the night encounters they favor. The shorter ranges of the bow were not such a problem in the dark. There was no muzzle flash to draw return fire, and the sound of the bow did not carry long distances. Harold, with his exceptional night vision, could easily hit targets 150 yards away in what mortals considered total darkness. His big, crank-operated three-hundred-pound crossbow could make shish kebabs out of two or three enemies standing too close together.

Phillips instructed Harold in conventional firearms as well, and he learned to use the rifle, the assault rifle, shot guns, pistols, and revolvers. At fifty yards, he could hit a paper plate with a .357 or .44 revolver nine times out of ten. He could easily hit a man-sized target with a rifle at six hundred yards, sometimes at eight hundred yards. He showed him how to load his own cartridges with the same brass and to adjust charges by exact weight when precise fire was needed. This way, he learned how to conserve ammunition and get many more rounds for a lesser weight, reusing the same cartridge cases.

About Harold's work in marketing and business management, I will mention only that he did quite well and ranked in the upper half of this class when he graduated with his bachelor's degree.

III. THE WAGES OF SIN

Harold had already had his degree in six months and was looking for employment. It was tough in the tight economy back then. He had applied to dozens of employers online; heaven help anyone without computer skills today. Meanwhile, Julia kept busy operating the Love Ranch.

Julia was working on her accounts one morning when the phone rang. She answered her telephone on the second ring.

"Hello, Julia Strange," said the voice on the other end. "This is Lugio Pescante from the Taxi Driver's Union. We need to have a talk. "

"About what?"

"About you continuing on with your business. If you want our taxi drivers to keep on bringing people to your brothel, you need to see me. Meet me tomorrow at the Tahiti Bar in the Golden Cornucopia, two in the afternoon."

"I'll be there."

Julia remembered Freemont Street looked a lot different when she had first come to Las Vegas years ago. Now it was the Freemont Street Experience arched over with thousands of lights controlled by computers that could make all sorts of pictures or spell out different messages. Relatively new were the zip lines installed as a ride for some of the more adventurous tourists.

The Golden Cornucopia occupied a prominent corner with its flashing sign, which depicted a seemingly endless flow of gold pieces from the cornucopia. Until after Big Richard's death, there had been a display of a million dollars in $500 and $1,000 bills, but now when the casino was not doing as well and the bills had become collector's items worth more than their face value, the exhibit had been taken down.

The bar was not particularly crowded; the tall bamboo stools under the fake palm leaf thatched roof only had two or three persons talking to a barman behind the bar who stood before the long mirror stretching its whole length. On one wall was a painting of half a dozen hula dancers against a lush tropical landscape. Julia had no sooner seated herself in a corner booth than Lugio appeared with two of his henchmen—with the union's treasurer and secretary.

"It's this way, Julie," he explained. "We don't think you are paying enough to our taxi drivers who bring out many of your customers. We think you should give each of them at least $1,000 for every customer he or she brings."

"Lugio, even although it's against the law, I don't mind paying out $100 just to keep friendly relations, but that's ridiculous, I couldn't pay that much."

"Then I think you should get out of the business of managing a cat house. I could suggest the name of someone who could bring in more cash and give you a nice cut. I mean, aside from your share from your own personal customers. Really, this kind of a business should be run by a man."

Julia felt a flush of anger and looked down, lest they see the flash of her eyes. Then she said, "You've been president of the union how for long, six months? You were nominated by the boys in Chicago, right? Well, Nevada is different, and so are the rules here. Prostitution is legal here, and it's a different game. If you leave us alone, then there's no problem. If you don't want to take customers to our house, well, the Taxi Authority might not be too happy, but I won't protest."

Lugio glared angrily at her, "If you don't give us what we want, I will tell every single guy who wants to visit you that your girls are all clapped up and all thieves, besides. I will also help out Pahrump's Society for Promotion of Public Virtue. I'll help them put you out of business."

"Those old biddies that are threatening to burn down my house? Don't make me laugh. Most of them are at least seventy years old. They are not going to burn anything down."

"Well, I might just give them a hand."

"Don't do that. If you do, I can't answer for your safety, not even your lives."

"Well, in Chicago, we know how to deal with uppity women. You could have had nice money. Tangle with me, and you'll have nothing."

Julia left then, knowing she would have to tighten up security or lose her business. She was certainly going to lose money because of the taxi drivers. She would have to be careful because if people came out to burn her house and ended up dead, that would be just what the people wanting to outlaw her place would need. She had to protect herself but with the least harm possible to others. First, she needed to hire a new bouncer and guard.

Harold finally landed a job as an account manager for an auto-leasing firm, and he hurried to let his aunt Julia know the good news. Since she was on duty at the office that day, he was beeped in to see her.

"Good news, Aunt Julia! I finally got hired," he said, "And the pay is not bad. By the way, who is the new guy at the gate? What happened to old Dan Furgeson?"

"He's working at the bar today," Julia said. "I had to put on some extra security."

"Not the SPPV again."

"No, it's the mobbed-up teamsters this time, not the biddies."

"Let's not think about them right now. Let's celebrate with a dinner and drinks on me," Julia said.

Julia took the day off, and her cook served them an excellent lobster dinner, complete with a delicious Piersporter wine. After several glasses together, Julia suggested Harold stay in his old room and not to return to town until later that night. Harold agreed and went off to bed in a room still surrounded by reminders of his youthful exploits, his high school pictures, and his diploma. There were crossed swords on one wall and a crossbow and quiver hung on the other. He went off to sleep at one in the afternoon, but stirred early in the evening. Then he heard an unmistakable sound—a gunshot.

Springing from his bed, he grabbed the bow and quiver, turned out the light over the entrance to the cottage, and plunged into the darkness. He could see that some people were firing on the guard at the gate of the brothel, not really trying to kill him, at least, not unless they were incompetent, but pinning him down. The new guard was returning the fire, evidently aiming toward the flashes. Then it occurred to Harold. This attack must be meant to keep the guard occupied while others attacked the brothel, perhaps trying to set it on fire.

Harold sped through the darkness over paths he had known since childhood, and skirting the main building, he spotted a group of six men approaching it from the rear, their hands full of bottles of gasoline stuffed with rags.

Rapidly he worked the windlass drawing back the powerful bow, then loaded the quarrel. The stupid gangsters were clearly visible, silhouetted by the lights from the bordello. He sighted and squeezed the trigger.

Thunk.

The rearmost of the group went down as the arrow passed straight through him, tearing an X-shaped wound. The others didn't notice. Harold reloaded, then sighted on a second man walking beside another. Again, his bow sounded, and the man staggered and fell against his companion.

"Hey, someone is shooting at us!" the man shouted and drew out his semiautomatic pistol. He looked around in vain for a target. "Rick! Rick is dead!" he shouted. Another man turned and started firing his assault rifle blindly in Harold's general direction.

Thunk.

"Ugh," he grunted as the arrow pierced him. Once more, Harold shot down a fourth enemy. The other two dropped their bottles and fled away from the buildings.

Harold swiftly followed and pulled down the hindmost man, ripping into his jugular and drained that man's blood. One man, and only one man, escaped, for the snipers firing at the gate guard discovered that the ex-marine could shoot and shoot well when he had muzzle flashes to aim at.

Julia had to call Delia and ask an unusual favor. For the first time ever, she would need a vampire clean up squad to remove the bodies and evidence of the attack. Thirty years later, young folks exploring the desert would find a long-abandoned mineshaft with human bones, whitened by time at the bottom. The Las Vegas police would be at a loss.

Lugio learned that the little lady at the Love Ranch could play rough. He decided that taking over her business was simply not worth it. There were easier targets, other brothels, massage parlors, outcall businesses, and the like. Julia now learned that $100 would once more be considered a sufficient tax on the wages of sin, so taxi service to her business was restored. This event thus ended Harold's first real mortal combat.

IV. His Sister's Sorrows

Mary Santiago had often wondered why her father had chosen to kill himself and abandon his children. Her mother, who was an attorney, had long ago left Las Vegas for suburban Virginia, near Washington, DC, where she worked as a lobbyist for the casino industry. While she loved her mother, Martha, and her brother, John, she was keenly disappointed in her womanizing father's suicide. Her mother had tried to be fair and not paint him in too dark a light, but still, it hurt that he had abandoned the three of them along with life itself. She heard she had a half-brother who had disappeared mysteriously with his mother Clarissa, a brother whose name she did not even know. These things Ernest learned from her book, *Tribulations of a Governor's Daughter*.

As a teenager, she had desperately tried to fit in, be popular, and had fallen in with a fast crowd, who knew how to take advantage of that. She fell for a lying, womanizing guy she thought was so wonderful and who left her pregnant at sixteen. After the abortion, she decided to be smarter and to concentrate on her studies. Since she was ambitious, it occurred to her that she should return to Nevada to enroll in its University's School of Hotel Administration and get a bachelor's degree that would be more useful than decorative.

Her first two years were successful, and she had a three-point-five average. The parties were great too, and she reconnected with people who knew her family well. School in Las Vegas was an undergraduate's dream. There were plenty of handsome guys, cool girls, and a great night life scene, places like the Flames of Love and the Bordello Club.

Mary and Janet Richards found that the Flames of Love seemed to have some of the handsomest, coolest guys, well dressed, and good dancers. Mary stood five feet three, with green eyes, short black hair, and a clear completion, while Janet was a tall red-headed girl with blue eyes, an oblong face and freckles, and wore her hair in a ponytail. On this Friday night, the salsa music was great, but Janet was sick.

"Let's go home," Mary said. "You look green."

"No, I'll get a taxi. I can't ruin my best friend's Friday."

"Don't be silly. Come home with me."

"Really, I'll be okay. Just have fun."

Mary accompanied her friend to the taxi stop and sent her home, then went back inside to rejoin the fun. Mary danced with several guys, a couple of them that she knew from school. Then a group of three came up to her table. The first young man was of average height, with black hair and brown eyes, and with him was a couple, the man who was not so tall and a thin blonde woman with short hair streaked with red.

"Hi, Mary. I'm Justin Phillips. Don't you have Ms. Harrison for economics?"

"Yeah, but I don't remember you."

"Well, with eighty students there, I'm not surprised. I remember you, however, because you usually sit behind Goth Girl. She of the piercings and black outfits."

Mary laughed. "That's right."

"I'd like you to meet my friends, Jake Hensley and Cat Jones."

"It's a pleasure to meet you."

The four of them joined enthusiastically in the next two dances and then sat out the third, talking about the prospects for Nevada University's basketball team.

"This year," Jake said, "I'm betting they'll be the best in the nation."

"No, maybe in the conference again, not in the nation. Not with our new coach," Justin observed.

Then Cat spoke up, "You know, we're missing First Friday, and all the cool arts programs. Why don't we take a break from the club scene and go take a look?"

"Great idea," Mary said. "Why not?"

"Why don't we all just go in Justin's car and bring Mary back afterwards?" Jake asked.

"Let's go then," Mary said.

Mary would have been a little frightened in the dark, almost deserted area in the parking garage where Justin had his car but felt secure going with her three new friends.

Justin got in to the silver Ford Taurus on the driver's side, Mary got into the passenger's seat, and the other couple got in the back.

No sooner had they closed the doors, Justin suddenly reached over and grabbed Mary around the neck with his right arm. "Let's have it," he said.

Jake passed him the cloth with the ether, and Justin pushed it down over the face to the struggling girl, managing to keep it there until Mary finally passed out.

Several minutes later, they had her gagged and tied up with rope and put her into the back part of the car. Justin started the engine and pulled out of the garage.

"Six million easy," he said. "That's what she's worth to us."

"That's two for each of us!" Cat exclaimed.

"Yeah, she even looks more like her mother than the Governor," Jake said.

"Smart idea, doctoring her friend's drink," Cat observed.

Harold finished a cup of coffee, straightened his tie, and opened the door of his apartment, 201B, in the Tuscan Villas, picked up the newspaper, then turned on his television for the early news.

"—And just breaking we have a story that the daughter of the late Governor Santiago has been kidnapped. It's reported the kidnappers are demanding an undisclosed ransom for her release." That got Harold's attention fast. Kidnappers had taken his half-sister and were demanding money. He had to find out who did it before it was too late. Kidnappers rarely released their victims, usually they just killed them once they had the cash.

Nevertheless, Harold put on his dark glasses and his hat and went down the steep narrow stairs that led to the ground level parking lot and his ride. Until he had seniority to ask for flexible work scheduling, he had to adapt his life to the daily cycle of most humans. Anyway, he could see that he would need the night for more important tasks, at least right now.

At dusk, Harold headed for the Bordello Club, for a word with Delia. He found Delia in her office, where she worked from time to time when not on the floor. He had some important questions for her. "Delia, I urgently need to know what was going on at the Flames of Love with Mary Santiago. I know that our crew there is smarter than to target a celebrity."

"That would violate my orders. The girls we take are never famous and are usually completely unknown. The staff there knows that, and we have never had anyone break our rules. We never kidnap anyone for money. We seek only blood and sometimes workers. This has to be the work of humans."

"Would it be possible for me to see any video tapes of the action there on Friday night?"

"The police have already asked for the tapes, but we made copies, of course. None of our vampires came near her as far as I can tell, but Mary danced with a series of human partners and left with three of them. We have pictures of them going into the parking garage, and then, they disappear."

"I need a note from the manager giving me clearance to follow up on this investigation," Harold said. "I want to see all the tapes, not just what the police took, and every car that entered or left the garage that evening. Also I need permission to talk with all of the staff on duty that night."

"None of that should be a problem. I don't want suspicion falling on us because of this case, and I understand your interest in rescuing your sister. Fortunately, their greed has led them to make at least one mistake. If they had waited a week, we would have erased the tapes."

Harold spent a seemingly fruitless hours at the Flames of Love talking to the staff, vampires and humans. He viewed the videotapes of the group entering and leaving the casino.

Unfortunately, the car had been parked in a poorly lighted, less-used area in the garage. Mary had hung out mainly with the college crowd. Several witnesses remembered seeing Mary with another couple, but nothing stuck out. Everyone except Mary had paid cash. Harold went home vowing to return for further investigation next evening. There must be some clue as to the identity of the criminals.

Harold visited Aunt Julia on Sunday talk about the kidnapping. She was very sympathetic and observed that it was really unfortunate that Janet got sick that evening.

That bothered Harold, and he considered that for a long while.

On Monday evening, Harold returned to the Flames of Love and talked to the bar staff. Just who had served the drinks to Mary and Janet? Of course, the barman had recognized Mary from television coverage during her father's governorship. They were all a little excited about serving a celebrity. One of the cocktail waitresses had quit the following day because she had decided she would move on the Atlantic City. Yes, she had been the one who served the drinks to the girls. There was even some tape from the "eye in the sky," but nothing that looked suspicious. The waitress's final check had not been sent out, however, and there was an address for her on record.

Early next evening, Harold went out to the apartment complex where Anne Johnson lived. He knocked on the door.

"Anne? Anne Johnson?"

"Yes?"

"I'm here about your paycheck. May I come in?"

"Sure."

Harold stepped inside her threshold, saw a woman with long blond hair and a full figure, then fixed his eyes on hers. "You were really working for someone else when you were at the Flames of Love, right?"

Anne felt those terrible eyes boring right into her brain and said, "I just got a couple of bucks for helpin' out. I never did a thing to hurt the club."

"What did you do and who paid you?"

Those red eyes just compelled her to speak though her mind screamed otherwise. "It was Jake. He used to pay me $100 extra just to put pills into girls' drinks and make them giddy, so he could screw 'em. Girls disappear all the time at the Flames, and no one sees it. So it was good money. This time, he gave me $200, but he said nothin' 'bout kidnapping the girl. When I found out who it was and what happened, I just freaked and wanted to leave town."

"Who is this Jake, and what does he have to do with the club?"

"Jake Zachery, he calls himself, and he hangs with Justin. Sometimes with a girl Cat or Cate or something like that and knows me and my friend, Mike, who sometimes works the bar."

"What does Jake look like?"

"He's tall, black haired, and hot. Why he needs drugs to get girls, I don't figure."

"Come, now. Submit," the vampire urged. Anne stood on wobbly legs, her body moving unwillingly toward the vampire.

Harold seized her, slashed open her throat, and drank until she felt faint. He licked her neck to heal the wound.

"Listen, Anne, tomorrow morning, without fail, you will go to the police and volunteer all the information you told me and anything else they ask. Do that and you live. Try to run and you die. I know your taste and smell. Now you will forget me completely but not my warning. You will go to the police, and you will live."

Harold dropped the fainting girl onto a sofa, then turned, and left the way he came. This was the first time he had tried to plant that kind of command for future action. Would Anne obey? He had asked the staff at the club to hold her check a couple of days, but would that be enough to keep her from fleeing in panic?

All night long, he lingered in the darkness within sight of her place, but he would have to withdraw with the dawn; he was expected elsewhere during the day. So far, she had not stirred from her apartment.

That evening, the story was on the news. A mysterious new witness had appeared with information about the kidnapping. The police were seeking three persons of interest, two males and one female. Some people who had worked at the bar in the Flames of Love were interviewed by police. Harold was very happy the waitress had felt compelled to go to the police.

The kidnappers didn't take this news so well.

Justin was furious. "We paid that bitch good money to drug the girls and now the police know. How are we going to shut her up?"

"Call up Mike and tell him if his friend doesn't clear out of town now, she's dead meat." Jake said.

"Why don't we just kill the bitch?" Cat advised. "By the way, how's our little princess?"

"Scared shitless," Justin answered. "So far, her mother hasn't answered our note."

"I know just how to fix that," Jake said. "Let's talk to her."

The kidnappers went into the bedroom of the apartment where Mary was tied up hand and foot and gagged. "Take off the gag," Justin commanded. Jake untied and removed it from her mouth.

"How are we doing today, princess?" Jake said.

"Please let me go. Just let me go. I won't say a word." Two wide, green eyes looked out from her frightened, pale white face as her trembling lips pled with them for her life.

"So far, we have no indication that your mother will pay the ransom. I'm going to need a piece of you. So decide, will you give me an ear or a finger?"

"Please…please…don't disfigure me."

"That's a woman for you, always worried about her looks," Justin said.

"So it will be a finger then. I'll make it a little finger this time."

"Gag her and blindfold her first," Justin said. "I don't want to hear her screams."

Jake gagged Mary again, then bound a handkerchief over her eyes. Then he went to fetch his hatchet.

Afterward, Jake told Cat the instructions of the ransom note. "Send the ransom as directed. If you don't, you'll get your daughter back free—one piece at a time." Cat had put on rubber gloves to cut out letters one by one from the newspaper and paste them onto the blank page. "Put that in the box with her finger, and we'll send it from the main post office," Justin declared.

That night, Harold took up his position in an apartment across the street from Anne's place. He noticed that the police were patrolling the area; two cars went by in an hour. There was no other unusual activity then. Nothing had been released about the police informant.

It was one o'clock in the morning, just after a police patrol car passed, a van parked on the street, and three figures emerged and made their way toward the building where Anne lived. Harold was out of the apartment door, down the stairs, and into the street in a flash, but he moved cautiously and quietly then. The three looked around to confirm that all was quiet and then entered the building. Harold followed, but not too close. When they stepped onto the elevator, he waited until the doors closed, then took an adjoining elevator to the floor above and started down the stairwell. He paused in the hall just around the corner from Anne's apartment.

"For the last time, Anne, open your door. If you try to call anyone, we'll kill you right now," Jake added. "Come with us, and we won't hurt you."

Harold rounded the corner in a moment. His .44 pointed straight at the center of the group. "Hands up now!" he said.

Jake reached into his pocket for a gun.

Blam! roared the .44, and Jake jerked back against the wall and then fell.

The rest of the kidnappers put their hands up.

Harold made them lean against the wall while he made a quick search and came up with a couple of pistols, a .40 caliber weapon and a .380 caliber automatic in the woman's purse.

"Where is Mary?" he demanded.

"At the apartment," Cat said.

"Get the keys," Harold said, looking straight at the woman.

Anne opened her apartment door cautiously and peeked out around the security chain.

"Anne, call 911 and get the police, and an ambulance here as fast as possible. You just shot this guy who was about to kidnap you. That's all you remember. Here, take this .44."

Anne looked at Harold's eyes and said, "Yeah, that's what happened. I shot Jake."

"You two, let's go to the apartment—now!" Harold motioned to them with the .40 caliber automatic.

They went back to the van, and Harold made Justin drive back to the apartment where they were holding Mary.

Harold found Mary tied up, numb with fear, after being brutalized and raped by the kidnappers. When he saw her missing finger, he felt a rising flush of anger.

"Thank God," she said. "Nobody seemed to care. Not my Dad, who killed himself, not even Mom. Everyone abandoned me to this…this horror."

He untied and released her, but he told her, "Stay here a moment." *These criminals deserve to die*, he thought. They would have killed Mary when they got their hands on the cash. There was a camera with pictures of the current newspaper, and a terrified Mary holding up her left hand with its severed finger.

He motioned the kidnappers into the next room. He made the woman sit in a chair while he covered her with the pistol. Quickly, he extended the pistol toward her and straightened his arm, then fired twice at her chest. She jerked up and fell from the chair. Justin stood with a stupid expression on his face as Harold turned quickly and fired the .380 automatic at his face. Then he too fell. Harold placed the .380 into the hand of Cat and bent her fingers around it, pointed it toward the roof, and pulled the trigger. Justin got the .40 caliber pistol, which indeed had been his, and fired once toward the wall behind Cat.

Harold went back to Mary, looked into her eyes, and he told her, "You heard the kidnappers arguing about who would get the largest share of the ransom. Then the firing began. You worked your hands free of the ropes and escaped, came in the other room, and found both kidnappers dead, then you called 911. You remember nothing more, except this. Your father never deserted you. He was murdered. For all his many faults, he did love his children. Remember he loved you, and that his suicide was faked. Now lie down a moment and compose yourself. You are alone." Harold left the apartment and headed home.

Heiress Mutilated, Kidnappers Killed proclaimed the headlines of the *Las Vegas Review Journal*, and all the local television channels were talking about the kidnapping for the next week. There was a long interview with Mary on television in which she explained what she heard of the deadly confrontation between the kidnappers in the other room and how she managed to work free of the ropes and call police after the shooting. The district attorney charged Anne for her role in drugging Mary but conceded her shooting of Rodger Hernandez, who went by the name Jake, might have been justified. When Rodger recovered after surgery, he told an incoherent tale of being shot by a red-eyed, fanged monster. Medical doctors concluded that drugs might have caused his delusions

THE TRIUMPH OF HAROLD HALBMANN

I. COUNTING KINGS

After stopping the attack on his aunt Julia and rescuing his half-sister, Mary, from kidnappers, the vampire Harold Halbmann reflected on his mission and began to think that he needed to know more about his father than his aunt had told him. Perhaps Uncle Ernest could provide a fresh perspective on his father and his murder. So one evening after work, he dropped by unannounced on his uncle's place, at the suburban house where he lived. Uncle Ernest's house was the only one in the neighborhood, which defied the Water Authority's pressure to rip out all the grass and substitute a gravel lawn and water-saving desert plants. The lawn was a lush green in the spring and fall and a bit brown in the winter and the raging heat of summer. This fall, it soon would be green when the roses were in full bloom, but it was still a bit brown when Harold rang the doorbell.

Ernest who stood about five foot seven was wearing a guayabera shirt over khakis when he came to the door. He looked remarkably fit thanks to vampiric restoration, but he had dyed the hair gray at the sides so as not to cause too many comments by his neighbors. Although he had always walked, people probably thought he spent hours at the gym now.

"Uncle Ernie, how are you doing, and how is your mother?"

"We are both fine. How is your job working out? "

"Great. No problems at all with it."

"What brings you here today? "

"I want the hear more about my father, his friends, and how He Whose Name No Mortal May Speak murdered them. Aunt

Julia told me a good deal, but I would like to know a lot more. First, just how did my dad become famous?"

"Your father was Cuban American. His family fled to Miami after Fidel Castro established his Communist regime in Cuba. They had been upper middle class attorneys, but they came to the United States with little more than the clothes on their backs and a few valuable Roman gold coins from your grandfather Enrique's collection they smuggled out.

"When they settled in Miami, Florida, Enrique discovered that a Cuban law degree was worthless here. Cuban law is based on Roman law, United States law on English common law. Enrique had to start all over again, to support himself, his wife Evangelina and Samuel, his son who was born only six months after they came here.

"Luckily, Enrique had studied English and mastered it so well he was able to work as a court translator, first for Florida and then for the federal courts. He translated the words of many a drug lord into English for the courts, and he was paid quite well for it.

"He put your father and his younger sister and brother through the university. Your dad chose to attend Stanford in California. After Sam graduated and passed the bar exam, he found California had more lawyers than it needed and came to Nevada. After working as a criminal defense attorney, he managed to get a job with the Clark County DA in Las Vegas and rose quickly after his role in some high-profile cases. I don't think he ever believed in the possible innocence of the pair he charged with Big Richard's murder. He just took one shortcut too many.

"Richard York, the yuppie vampire from New York, was largely responsible for Sam's death. Richard saw Sam was a rising star and turned him and encouraged him to court your mother. If Sam hadn't become a vampire, he would have wound up disbarred, with a suspended sentence or, at worst, with a year or two of prison, and that would have been it.

"Your father could have never hid his identity as an immortal in prison and because our prime directive is to never make ourselves known to humans, he had to die. All his close associates had to go too, for the same reason, even poor Julia's husband. So the King's act was more an execution than a murder, although our kings are often arbitrary and cruel. The best thing is to have as little to do with them as possible."

Harold scratched his head at this, and after a moment, he asked, "Just who are these kings, are why are they like that?"

"I know you are not as fond of history as I am, so instead of really explaining the past, I'll just get you to do the math. In four thousand years, there have been just twelve kings of all the vampires of whom we know, and all of them except one were killed by their successors. So then, the average king reigns a little over three hundred years. The kingship comes at a high price. In the last reign alone, four hundred pretenders challenged the King to formal battle, a little over one a year. All except for the one who is now King died in personal combat. And these figures don't include several thousands the King ordered killed because he suspected they were plotting to seize the crown. Informers surround the kings like a cloud and their whispers are fatal to many an innocent person. 'Uneasy lies the head that wears the crown…'"

"One king though was killed by someone other than a rival?" Harold asked.

"That's right. A mortal woman, angry because the King had drained her husband, staked our third King, and cut off his head one afternoon as he napped. Ever since, the kings have all appointed twelve mortals to guard them during the day, of which at least six stand watch in times of danger and three at all other times. The king himself draws their names from a vase every morning, the same day they go on watch. They first stand watch when eighteen, and they retire at thirty. The king then turns the best and makes them satraps for distant provinces. If he suspects any of disloyalty, he kills not only them but their wives, children, or parents."

"Who guards him at night?"

"Six friends accompany him to witness his acts and protect him from multiple attacks, but kings know how to defend themselves. They *are* kings exactly because they are the most powerful immortals. I will tell just one thing. Keep well clear of the King, and you can be around for many centuries."

"Why must we conceal our identity from mortals at all costs?"

"Harold, in medieval times, there were some immortals in southern France who grew just a little too sure of themselves. They were lords who had castles and lands and serfs to work those lands and lived openly as immortals. Some mortals even said it was better to work for vampire lords than regular mortal ones because immortals demanded a smaller share of the crop, but they did collect a blood tax. For most mortal serfs, this just meant a vampire would drink from them from time to time. In a few cases, for special celebrations, however, immortals took the life of a serf, usually a man. The vampire lords understood this meant a real loss to the human community and cost money for themselves too, and they allowed relatives to say good-bye to the condemned, share a final meal, and even encouraged their wives to have sex with them to try and produce children, to replace them. Then, after a few days, they stripped the man and cut his throat at the banquet, so that all might feast. If his widow had a child afterwards, her lord sent special presents as compensation for having no husband. A few reckless lords even sacrificed infertile couples for such parties, but even vampires considered that excessive.

"Local lords were jealous of the vampire rulers because they ruled long, consolidated and didn't have to divide their estates, so these malcontents went to the bishops who declared vampires creatures of hell and preached a crusade against them. They attacked the vampires, broke through the walls of their castles, killed the human guards and peasants, as well as the vampires, raped their women, and burned the castles and their villages to the ground. These areas became known as the burnt zone. In short, they nearly exterminated all of our kind in those parts and the survivors vowed never again to make themselves known to mortals; whoever does must die."

"Who was Richard York before Delia turned him?" Harold inquired, a bit weary of too much history.

"Richard, whose parents are well-heeled, was a sophomore at New York University, who hung out with his friends in Greenwich Village's Washington Square. He used to come to Vegas a couple of times a year when his parents indulged him with a personal vacation.

"Richard became an ambitious vampire, as ambitious as he was when mortal, and that got him killed. He was "Eternal Protector of the Southern Realm," for all the good it did him, and might have hoped to be satrap somewhere one day, but he just got himself killed. Stay away from the kings, I repeat myself, but the advice is good."

Harold thought this over and realized that the problem was not so much that the king was an evil murderer as that the whole system sucked. Although the system insured that the strongest vampires would be kings, it did nothing to insure that kings would administer justice fairly or help the vampire community as a whole or establish fair relationships with the human world. Instead, the kings spent their time trying figure out who would come forward to challenge them and killing would-be pretenders before they could force a personal response. In short, the vampire kingship sucked. Still, the king had done him, the Smith family, Aunt Julia, and those he executed great harm—evil that cried out for revenge. Even Aunt Julia, always kind and usually forgiving, burned with rage. His father was spared baking in the desert because a governor couldn't just vanish, he supposed. Did they show any mercy at all on his mother or only ultimate cruelty? All this would have to wait.

"Sufficient unto the day is the evil thereof." In other words, don't look for trouble. That's what Ernest often said. *Where did he get that anyway? Shakespeare? The Bible?*

Reading's not my thing, Harold mused. Other problems awaited his attention now.

11. When a Cornucopia Is Not So Golden

Hard times came to Las Vegas, a city once believed recession-proof. You could see it at the airport where fewer travelers came to the city. Unfortunately for Jim Smith, Clarissa's younger brother and now chief operating officer for the Golden Cornucopia, he faced a financial dilemma. The aging casino needed renovation everywhere, and that took cash. Banks were reluctant to loan money, especially when revenues were falling. In a desperate, short-sighted effort to raise cash, Jim had sold the World Tournament of Poker, the casino's most popular event, one that had drawn visitors for years, to a casino on the more modern strip. He even sold the famous million-dollar display since the collector value of its rare banknotes far exceeded its face value, but he still was having trouble raising the fifteen million dollars needed to completely redo all the hotel rooms and the casino floor. The Culinary Union, controlled by the Teamsters, was making things worse by demanding huge increases in wages for all its employees.

On that September day, clouds covered the sky in a solid overcast, and then suddenly, the rain came down in sheets for the first time in a year. It was as though a giant bucket had been turned upside down in the heavens above the city. The streets quickly filled with muddy water, and detention basins soon overflowed right afterward. Streets were awash with moving water and in some parking lots cars bobbed like fishing corks. Several people had to be rescued from their stranded cars using helicopters, and one man was swept into a wash and drowned.

Jim sat behind his desk, the same huge, antique one, which had once been Big Richard's and stared out the window at the gray sky watching as gusts of wind blew raindrops spattering against the panes of glass. Overhead, a neon fixture buzzed with two bulbs providing bright light for him to read the dismal news. Jim was a big man, over six feet tall, and in fact, most Smiths tended to grow up rather than out. Maybe it was part of their Colorado and Montana heritage. Some had been famous gamblers in the frontier towns, others had bet on copper mines, and they had struck it rich. The Vegas Smiths sprung from those Smiths who had run gaming even before it was legalized. Big Richard had favored Western attire—a Stetson, cowboy shirts, jeans, and boots—and his hat still hung from the hat rack by the office door. Jim wore a well-tailored suit and tie instead, framing his angular face.

Suddenly, the phone buzzed. Jim picked it up. "Jim speaking."

"Mr. Smith, this is John Massimo, and I believe that we could really help you and your business. I think it would really be useful for us to get together this week. Is there a day that would be convenient?" Now Jim had heard that John had been quite successful in aiding other casinos in difficulty, so he thought it would be wise to see what he offered.

"Yes, I could meet you here in my office Wednesday or Friday. Would nine o'clock Wednesday work?"

"Fine, I'll see you then."

John appeared on schedule dressed splendidly in an expensive suit an immaculate white shirt with a silk tie and gleaming leather shoes.

"Good morning," John said. "I trust everything is going well with you."

"Just fine," replied Jim, "and I hope you are well too. I hear your businesses are really doing well these days."

John was black haired and brown eyed, a much shorter, heavier man, reaching only to Jim's chin. The latter stood up to greet him. He waved John to a vacant chair, and both men sat down. Although not really educated, Massimo had always admired those who were, and he aped their manners and copied their speech.

John started the conversation. "I have an offer, which I think would be mutually profitable to both of us."

"I know you've been looking for a loan to refurbish the Cornucopia Hotel and Casino. Exactly how much would it take?"

"We need fifteen million dollars to update and redo all the rooms in the hotel, to convert all remaining slots to cashless, modernize our sports book and kitchens."

"If I could get you the money and for only two points above prime, would you consider a deal? And," said John with a dismissive wave of his hand, "what if I could make your problems with the Culinary Union go away?"

"How would you do that?"

"I have good connections with the union, people who know how to convince them to do what is in their long-term interest. After all, unless your casino prospers, they'll all have no jobs."

"What would you ask in return for all of this?" Jim asked, getting to the bottom line.

"Well," John replied, "of course, my investors would expect the prime rate plus two points on the loan. Also, I would want a concession for a gift shop and the right to name three employees at your casino, men who would look after our interests."

"And these guys you would place in our casino, they would all have gaming licenses, right?"

"My people will all pass the strictest scrutiny. You will have nothing to fear from the Gaming Commission."

"Would you give me a week to think about your proposal?"

"Take all the time you need, Jim, then call me and let's do the deal. When we sign, let's throw a party to celebrate our new partnership. Just give me a call when you are ready." With that, John rose and extended his hand to Jim.

Within a week, Jim was breathing easier. The deal was signed and sealed. In return for accepting a couple of new employees and a gift shop concession, he had the loan he needed and could fix up his casino. His big problems had a solution, and the Golden Cornucopia would once more know its former glory. Already, the head of Local 666 of the Culinary Union had agreed to reopen stalled negotiations on the basis of Jim's last proposal.

Really, Jim thought, *John has just as much influence as he was rumored to have.*

Everyone respected him, whether legitimate or mobsters. He was perfect man for any job, except for those requiring a gaming license. He had had some brushes with the law when a young man, he said. It was nothing serious, but the record just wouldn't go away. He had a charming manner that just made everyone see reason; in short, he was the perfect dealmaker.

The following spring, the renovation of the casino was well under way, and new contracts with the Culinary Union had saved millions. Floor by floor, workmen were repainting, redoing the bathrooms, and putting in new carpets in the hotel rooms. They had already replaced all the old coin operated slots. No longer did you hear the ding-ding-ding and fall of coins when the slots paid out to lucky gamers. Everything seemed to be going very smoothly. The new employees worked very well with the existing staff. Well, the economy was still not recovering fully. Jim was disappointed by the lower revenues from gaming operations, but soon, Jim mused, things would improve. Other casinos were already doing better, and there was no reason the Golden Cornucopia shouldn't be getting better results soon.

III. An Everyday Tragedy

The accident was a tragedy for sure, Harold thought. The worst of it was that Jim's daughter, Patricia, was dead. She was pulled from the wreckage of her Porsche after a head-on crash. The television channel had pictures of the twisted aftermath which resulted when eighteen-year-old Viernes Gonzalez's Mercedes Sports Utility Vehicle entered I-95 going the wrong way, causing several vehicles to swerve off the highway, and then smashing head on into Pat's car. The television caught the ambulance crew helping Viernes from the wreckage, almost unscathed from the fatal accident. They took Pat to the morgue.

All the following week, the television carried fresh news about the collision. Viernes tested positive for not only alcohol but also for marijuana. Reporters were waiting to see if the DA was going to charge her with driving under the influence leading to death or reckless driving. Viernes could face substantial prison time because of the fatality the newscast noted.

Rudolfo, Viernes' father, not only owned the Garden of the Gods strip club but two taxicab companies and a string of quasi-legal massage parlors that were also fronts for prostitution within the city limits where that had been banned since World War II. So wealthy were the Gonzalez clan that they were able to completely defeat every attempt by the city authorities to close down the illegal operations. There was little doubt that his relationship with the city and county had been sweetened by generous cash gifts to city councilmen and county commissioners.

Within a day, Viernes left the hospital. In fact, her injuries amounted to no more than a few scrapes and bruises. The DA's office hinted that it would bring a charge of reckless driving against Viernes, a much less serious offense.

Meanwhile, the Smith family gathered to bury Jim's daughter Patricia in the Catholic cemetery. Jim was completely distraught when interviewed by reporters from Channel 13.

"I can't understand why nothing is happening in this case," he said. "I understand that young people make mistakes, but this was so outrageous, so incredibly stupid. I just don't see why the district attorney isn't charging the one responsible. Pat was the light of my life, and the hope of my family and now she is gone forever."

Two more weeks went by without action, then Jim called reporters to announce that he and the Smith family were going to bring suit against Viernes Gonzalez for ten million dollars, and indeed, the very next day, the Smiths' lawyers filed a wrongful death suit. Two days later, Viernes filed for bankruptcy although she had always been believed to be a wealthy heiress. The Gonzalez family had arranged that Viernes's money would evaporate, but she could still live in comfort in the family mansion. Nor did the young lady slow down her fast lane life in the least. She was partying at the Palms and in every celebrity venue, just as if nothing had ever happened. Only now her family sent a driver and a bodyguard who accompanied her on her adventures.

Harold thought that it was totally wrong that Viernes would go Scott free after causing the death of an innocent member of his family. He considered long and hard what he should do; how might he punish her. He would have to neutralize her guards, but then what should he do? Then too, she was a celebrity, so he couldn't make her just disappear, or could he?

Things were really hopping at the Flames of Love that Friday night. Fridays were always the busiest nights at the club. The dance floor was filled with couples moving to the latest salsa beat; overhead hung a glittering mirror ball. Mini-skirted waitresses circulated along the edge of the crowded floor with trays of drinks for those seated at the tables. The night was young when Viernes, Adriana, and Maria made their way to a booth on one side of the floor, close to the band that was playing the music.

"What a hot club!" said Adriana, tossing her black hair to one side and surveying the room with her brown eyes. "This place has the sexiest men in Las Vegas, I believe. It nice you're back with us, Viernes. You've been missing the best action in town!"

Adriana had an olive completion, was short, and well endowed, while Maria was the tallest, a slender, small-breasted blond with short hair, and Viernes was of medium height, with an oval face, blue eyes and brown hair flowing to her shoulders and nice breasts. They were dressed for the occasion. Adriana wore a black outfit, a revealing halter top cut down to the navel, hot pants, and thigh-high fishnet stockings, high heels. Maria was dressed in a gray-and-black striped knee-length tube dress. Viernes, always the one to stand out, was wearing a magenta halter minidress slashed to the navel, knee-high black fishnets, and silver high heels.

"Let's order drinks," Maria suggested. "The night is young, and we are here for fun!"

"Yeah!" said Viernes with enthusiasm, motioning to a cocktail waitress.

"Three Bloody Marys on me!" she said.

"You were sure lucky," Adriana said, looking at Viernes. "You walked away from your accident without a scratch. And the law didn't charge you with anything. Amazing!"

"And it never will. We Gonzalez know how to make our luck, especially my dad. He does just what he pleases, and so do I." She smiled.

"Wow, that's neat," said Adriana, another wild child, who had had a few drug arrests herself including a DUI.

The waitress arrived with the drinks, and the three women took them and started to drink them.

Just then, a group of three guys approached the girls to introduce themselves.

"You three ladies look hot. These are my friends, Joe and Sam, and I'm Jack," Harold said. "And you are?"

"Viernes. The tall one is Maria. The *chiquita* is Adriana."

"Why don't we hit the floor? It's a shame to lose this music."

"Good idea," Viernes said and set her almost empty glass on the table.

Two hours of dancing and drinking later, they all were sitting at the table in a mellow mood.

"You know, you are so great. It would be great to slip away and just be alone together," Jack said. "I hear there is a great view of the city at night from Mount Charleston."

"Yeah," Viernes said. "It might be fun for us to go there, but we wouldn't be alone with my driver and guard."

"Aren't they waiting over at the bar?" Jack asked. "Couldn't we just slip away for an hour or two in my ride, return in two or three hours without them being any wiser?"

"Sounds like fun," Adriana said, smiling mischievously as she looked at Joe.

"Let's do it!" Viernes said.

They went to the parking garage got in the SUV and drove up the narrow road to Mt. Charleston. And on the road from Kyle Canyon to the Ski Lodge, they found an overlook with a wonderful view of the city below. After looking out over the city a few moments, everyone got back into the vehicle.

"You know you are really spectacular," said Jack and leaned over to kiss Viernes.

She replied, "You're pretty hot too." She her hands up around his neck to return his kiss with interest. Soon, they were lost in their embrace and oblivious to the world. The other guys took their cue from Jack, and they gave their whole attention to the women.

Soon everyone was excited as the men caressed the girls and their hands went everywhere. There was just enough room in the vehicle to make out. Sighs and moans followed and then—

Harold bit Viernes's throat, and the other vampires attacked the two other girls. Harold drank deep but did not kill Viernes. He was a little tipsy from the alcohol content of her blood. The other vampires fed well also. Then Harold drove the vehicle back down to Charleston Village where there was an unoccupied cabin sometimes used in the summertime. They took Viernes and her friends inside.

When Viernes woke up on the bed, she found her hands tied. There was no trace of her friends. The vampires had erased their memories and left them in a confused state on the strip.

"What happened? Where am I?" Viernes felt so tired and confused. She was looking straight into the red eyes of a fanged creature. A vampire, she realized.

"You are with me," Harold said, "where you will remain the rest of your life, a life destined to be short."

"Your recklessness cost the life of an innocent girl, and you have showed no trace of remorse, no regrets at all. For that, you will die after furnishing me a meal or two. Meanwhile, think about what you have done, ask God for a pardon, if you believe in him."

"Don't kill me. I'm sorry, I really am. It's just that Maria brought me this grass, and we just had to enjoy it, but then, I needed to get home, but I'm sorry the other girl died."

"Don't blame others, Viernes. Accept responsibility yourself. Anyway address your regrets to your God, not me. Do you even know the name of the girl you killed?"

"No, I just can't remember. I was pretty messed up."

"Well, I think you should know her name before you die. It was Patricia, Patricia Smith, daughter of Jim Smith. Think about the life you took and the harm you caused another family."

Harold turned and walked out of the room into the kitchen where he prepared a meal for Viernes. Not anything fancy, hot dogs, and mashed potatoes with cranberry juice.

He brought her in and made her eat to help her regain some of the damage from blood loss. After all, she would be his lunch and supper. She ate in silence.

"Please," she said afterward. "I don't want to die. Let me live."

"Too late," he said. "Talk to your God, not me."

Saturday night came, and Harold realized it was time. He had fed well from the guilty girl and served her enough food to partially replace the blood he took, and now it was time to end her life. Monday he would have to be back at his office.

"Please don't kill me," Viernes pleaded when Harold came into the bedroom where he was holding her.

"I suppose I could have just let you be. Sooner or later, if you kept up your crazy behavior, you'd kill yourself. The problem is, you might kill another person or two first. That, I won't allow."

"Please, please let me live. Don't kill me."

"That's already been decided, but I'm offering you one last chance to apologize to those you hurt and to say good-bye to your parents. You don't have to if you don't want to, but you can if you wish. There is a pencil and paper on the table."

She took the paper, stared at it a long while, then wrote, "Mom, Dad I'm sorry my life has to end. I regret very much killing Pat the way I did. I was just so stupid. Now it's too late."

Harold took the paper, folded it somewhat awkwardly with his latex gloved hands, and put it into his pocket. Then he set a plate of food and a glass of juice before her.

"Eat, take your time. I won't send you out of this world without a good meal in your stomach."

Viernes ate slowly and then looked at the empty plate.

Harold said, "Sorry, Viernes, but it's time to go." Then he took her out of the cottage to his car and to her fate.

⸎

This disappearance of Viernes and her companions had caused her guards to nearly panic when they could find no trace of her. They went to where they had parked, and there was no vehicle. Had she taken off driving it in a drunken state? Her driver didn't think she had the keys, but he wasn't absolutely sure she didn't have a copy. She and her friends had been seen leaving the club and headed for the parking area. No one knew where they had gone.

Rudolfo Gonzalez called the police to report his daughter had disappeared, and her SUV was missing. He fired her driver and bodyguard on the spot when she didn't return home that day. Her mother was heartbroken.

What had happened to my little girl? she thought. The police put out an all-points bulletin for the SUV with a description and the license number, but nothing turned up.

※

Harold took Viernes and looked into her eyes. "You must never return to your parents again or all of you will die. You will remember only that you are Maria Gomez from Guadalajara. Here is your identification from the Mexican Consulate. Here is $100." He drove her to the Pale Angel Motel.

Harold's vampire allies, Delia and Bree, had removed the SUV from the casino to a place outside town, swapped the license plates of another vehicle of the same make and model, and driven it to the motel parking lot, where they repositioned the original plates.

Harold had registered at the motel, shown a false driver's license, and Viernes's real identification, to the clerk, then he returned to his vehicle, took Viernes down to Freemont Street. He put her on a bus to Los Angeles.

"Good-bye, Maria," he said, and then he turned and left her.

Harold took her wallet and cut up all the credit cards and her driver's license. Henceforth, Viernes would have to make her way through the world on foot. It was safer that way for everyone, Harold thought. The police found no other clues, no strange fingerprints, nothing else at the motel.

Rudolfo Gonzalez brought a wrongful death suit in the Nevada courts against James Smith for twenty million dollars, claiming that Viernes would never have committed suicide. It was against her religion. Either Jim had hired someone to murder his daughter, or he had harassed her with a frivolous lawsuit that drove her to desperation. Lawyers clashed in court, one side claiming that Viernes's bankruptcy was only an attempt by her family to shield her from responsibility and a lawsuit should go forward against her estate based on her holdings the previous year and the other that Jim had murdered or driven Viernes to the point of insanity.

It all made very good press and even better television, but it cost plenty on both sides. Eventually, both parties dropped the lawsuits against each other, rather than bankrupt themselves.

IV. If a Cornucopia Runs Dry

Jim had been so shaken by the death of his only daughter and its bitter legal aftermath that he had paid no attention to his business. Now three months after the death of Viernes, he was looking at the shocking figures showing that revenue from the Golden Cornucopia was down and costs up. At the very least, he would have to lay off employees. At this rate, he would have trouble paying off the loans that had made the renovation of the casino possible.

Meanwhile, at the casino coffee shop, John Massimo was meeting with his two agents in the hotel-casino. They settled into a corner booth well away from the hubbub. A well-dressed heavyset man with a just a little beard visible sat opposite John, and an equally well-dressed but taller blond man who sat to his right. They conversed with lowered voices.

Looking at the man sitting directly across from him, John said, "Pete, you guys have been taking too much off the top. We are going to have to cut the skim by half if we want to make sure the Golden Cornucopia survives."

"Look, John, that'll mean less money for all of us. We don't want to do that."

"Don't be like the stupid people in the fairy story who killed the golden goose. Jim has to be able to make his payments to the Teamster's Pension Fund and not only his neck but ours are riding on it. If we tried to take over the Cornucopia, the Gaming

Commission would smell a rat in ten seconds, and this whole sweet business would be over."

"In other words," said the blond fellow, "we will lose out unless we cut back. Since this is your idea, John, I think half the reduction should come from your share."

"It's important, so I'll do it."

Although Massimo and his confederates tried to carry out the planned reduction in the skim, they ran into problems, not so much with carrying out the reduction in payments to themselves but dealing with some of Jim's employees they had corrupted, who didn't like the ideas they might make less illegal cash. In vain, the conspirators pointed out that if the casino were to close or lose its license, everyone would be hurting.

In the end, it was Ralph Jones from the counting room who spilled the beans. Ralph had started to use drugs, and one day, Metro arrested him for possession. He probably would be going to jail and would lose his employment because the Cornucopia had a drug free policy for all employees. So he told the police he knew that there was illegal skimming going on at his place of employment.

The police alerted the prosecutor and the Gaming Commission who launched two independent investigations into Jones's claims. The police interviewed Pete Picolo and Rick Masterson, but they said Jones's claims were a ridiculous lie on the part of a desperate drug user. They could find nothing to confirm what Jones said, but they still had suspicions. Employees at the Cornucopia seemed reluctant to talk with police. Police knew part of this reticence was traditional. In Big Richard's Day, gamers didn't go to the police about card cheats. They simply beat them up and dumped them in a back alley. This had been part of the legacy from the days of illegal gaming when gamblers couldn't go to police. Still this reluctance to talk was troublesome.

The Gaming Commission found that all employees had been correctly licensed, but there was a fifteen-million-dollar loan from the Teamsters that looked suspicious. It might even be a conflict of interest because the Casino's Culinary Union was affiliated with the Teamsters. Strangely, the Culinary Union had backed off most of its demands and signed a contract favorable to the casino at the very time the loan was made. The members of the commission realized that while they had not found a fire, they certainly had discovered smoke.

Soon, the media got wind of this, and stories started to circulate about mob influence in gaming, particularly in Las Vegas. The federal authorities wanted to know just why the Teamsters had made such a loan. Their treasurer told investigators that it strictly had been a business decision and that the casino had been making its payments faithfully. There was talk of introducing a bill in Congress to outlaw loans of this type.

Harold was troubled by all this. Was his family in league with the Mafia? Who struck this deal and why? What could he do to protect his mortal family—rich perhaps, but as frail as all mortals can be.

Harold set out to investigate who was responsible for the predicament. Did Jim betray the Smiths by making a deal with criminals that would be grounds for revoking the license of the Golden Cornucopia, or did the mob somehow infiltrate without his knowledge? What could he, as a vampire, do about it?

Harold asked around and found out that certain new people had come on the staff since the loan was negotiated. A couple of them worked in the counting room. All were legally licensed employees, of course. A new gift shop had also opened in the Cornucopia. He decided that he needed to follow up his investigation. He thought he knew exactly what to do.

Next evening, a nervous Pete Picolo got into his Mercedes to head home from the executive car garage. He had been working late, trying to tie up any loose ends that could expose the skim racket at the Cornucopia. He started the engine and looked in the rearview mirror. He froze in horror. Two enormous red eyes stared at him. There was also a revolver pointed straight at the back of his head, and he could see a lead bullet in each of its chambers.

"Pete," said a quiet voice, "you will tell me everything you know about the skim, who is behind it and who is involved. You had better tell the whole truth. Now, turn around and look at me."

Pete turned and was drowned in the awful power of those eyes. He started talking, and he just couldn't shut up even if he wanted to.

"It was John Massimo who organized it," he said. "He got approval from the mob bosses, approached Jim Smith, and hired me and Rick to supervise the skim. We take the money off the top, thirty thousand a day before it's counted. Then we divide it four ways, including a share for the boys in Chicago. We also pay out cash to six employees in the counting room to keep quiet about it."

"Ralph Jones was your top guy, right?"

"Yeah, he distributed cash to five others."

"How much?"

"Two thousand a week to him, half that to the others."

"Did the others know you were in charge?"

"No, he was the go-between, but now, it's Richard Simons."

"You will give me the names of the other four, and after you do, I will leave you. You will go home and call in sick tomorrow. You will stay put until I call you and say go, and when I do, you will leave Las Vegas and Nevada, and you will never return. If anything you told me is wrong, you die. If you want to live, you wait until I command you to go, and you never look back. You will remember only my instructions, and you will live in fear."

"Understand?" asked the authoritative voice.

"Yeah"

A few minutes later, armed with those facts, Harold slipped from the car, leaving a stunned and dazed Pete to go home and cower in terror. Harold took his mini cassette recording back and copied it, and the next day, he placed it in an envelope marked, "To Jim Smith, Golden Cornucopia Hotel. Confidential." Harold was beginning to be able to read humans, and he had a definite feeling about Jim, but he wanted to be sure—absolutely sure—he was reading Jim right.

Two days later, John Massimo's cellular buzzed. John was enjoying his morning coffee at the coffee shop.

"Yeah, John speaking."

"This is Jim. Jim Smith. We have to talk today. Meet me at my office at 1:00 p.m. sharp."

"See you there," he said. And the connection was broken.

"Hello, Jim," John said that afternoon when he entered Jim's office.

"Sit down, John. When did I ever authorize you to steal from our casino? Just when? I borrowed money, made a loan through your contacts, and I have made every payment even though the casino is not doing so well." Jim shot a look of anger at the smooth criminal.

"That's a lie. That guy Jones is just a liar. You should know that."

"Is Pete a liar too?" Then he started the tape player.

Pete's voice filled the room. "It was John Massimo who organized it. He got approval from the mob bosses, approached Jim Smith, and hired me and Rick to supervise the skim. We take the money off the top, thirty thousand a day before it's counted. Then we divide it four ways, including a share for the boys in Chicago. We also pay out cash to six employees in the counting room to keep quiet about it." Then Jim stopped the machine.

"No wonder the Golden Cornucopia is struggling with you bleeding us dry. No more, that's enough. I can't go to the commission. We'd lose our license, but you...you'd go to prison. What you've stolen, you've stolen, but every one you made me hire and all those they corrupted, you're all out of here. Your gift shop concession is terminated. You'll sell it to Mary Santiago for a thousand bucks."

"A thousand, that's robbery! It's worth six times that, at least."

"Well, consider what you stole as a down payment, then."

"The boys in Chicago will never accept this."

"You mean the mob?"

"Yeah, they'll come after you."

"Well, tell your bosses that there are still men at this casino who remember the old days before we became legal. Rivals tried to kill Big Richard six times, and they did kill his wife. Tell them I'll never start violence. But warn them that even if they kill me, other members of my family will never rest until they're punished. We Smiths stick together. Now go, and I never want to see your face once you sell out to Mary."

John Massimo, known to some as Maximum John, turned and walked out of Jim's office.

That evening, Harold collected the tape of the two men's conversation from the bug he had left in Jim's office. Now he knew what to do; his instincts had proven right.

The next night, when John entered his apartment after a long day and turned on the light, he saw a figure standing so still it could have been a statue. Before he could move, it sprang suddenly into motion, seized him by the collar, and forced back against a wall with incredible strength. Those powerful eyes locked on to his, and he could not turn away.

"John, what are you planning against Jim? Tell me everything or die right now. Talk!" Harold shook him once.

"It's not me. It's my bosses in Chicago. A team is flying in next week, three o'clock next Tuesday, afternoon. Four guys, two snipers, and two backups."

"Who are they, John?"

"There's Sure Shot Blackmann, Alex Axle, Sniper Hernandez, and Icepick Towers."

"How good are they?"

"Sure shot and Sniper are ex-marines, guys who never miss their target and have high power rifles with scopes. The other guys will have AK-47s or AR-15s or something like that."

"Where will they be staying?"

"Silver Ingot Hotel, rooms 325 and 326."

"Come with me, John. You'll be my guest for lunch and dinner." Harold smiled revealing two very white fangs.

Sure Shot and the boys enjoyed first class on a very smooth flight to Las Vegas, and a limo was waiting to take them to their hotel. In the morning, they'd be picking up their equipment and finalizing their plans, but they wanted to kick back and pretend to be ordinary visitors for a few hours. They had no sooner settled into their rooms than there was a knock on the door. Icepick looked out and saw four beautiful ladies in evening dresses. He opened the door and said, "Yeah."

One lady said, "Maximum John thought maybe you could use a little company this evening. I'm Delia. Here's Bree. They're Georgina and Justina. John is footing the bill. Would you like a night out on the town, or shall we simply dine in."

"Why don't we just dine in?" Sure Shot suggested from inside the room. "After all, we have to get up early tomorrow."

"Yeah," the others echoed, lasciviously looking over the women and nodding their heads. What followed became one of the most famous vampire orgies and feasts in history.

"Come in then," Sure Shot suggested. They paired up and settled in on the couches and chairs in the suite's living room. And then, they ordered dinner and drinks from room service.

While waiting, the guys stole a kiss here and there. Once they had eaten, the men got busy kissing and their hands were soon all over the women, caressing them through their clothing and running their hands into the girls' bodices and up and under their short skirts.

"Wow!" said Alex as he pulled off Georgina's panties, while Bree was unzipping Rick's pants. Nobody wanted to wait until naked, and the men pressed forward, with all the group still in various stages of undress, until Justina tore into the jugular of Sure Shot, who hardly noticed in his excitement.

That morning before dawn, four well-fed vampires would leave, and a crew would remove four completely drained corpses.

A week later, a passerby would notice a naked corpse impaled at an abandoned construction site outside town. John Massimo was dead. Someone had trimmed a nine-foot sapling, sharpened one end to make a stake, greased it and planted its butt firmly in the ground near a half-finished building. Then he had sat John Massimo on it, still alive, hands tied behind him, and run him down until the stake tore through his intestine. The stake was bloody. John had tried to push himself up off it repeatedly but could get not traction on the greased pole. Each time he tried to push up, more of his blood ran down the pole. Blood ran down the inside of his thighs, his leg, and dripped from his bare toe, making a puddle on the ground beneath it. *It was a language*, Harold believed, *that the even boys in Chicago could understand.*

V. ERNEST FRANK

When Ernest awoke from his afternoon nap, as evening shadows began to fall, he was startled by a sudden knock at the door. He looked through the peephole, and saw two enormous guys, who each must have stood six foot six inches tall and weighed at least 220 pounds each standing before his door.

"Open! Open in the name of His Majesty, the King!"

Cautiously, Ernest opened the door. These looked like the same enforcers who had visited him after the death of Sam.

"Good evening," he said. "How may I help you?"

One of the two shoved him and pushed him back into a chair.

"We hear you may be having improper contact with mortals," the vampire said. "Besides that, we need to know where Clarissa Santiago's child is."

"All I know," Ernest said as he felt his blood freeze in terror "was that Clarissa and her child disappeared the same night her husband died. As for mortals, I have the same necessary contact that we all have with them, no more."

"Yeah, and besides that, you take care of your mother. She will notice you are younger looking and will wonder why. What will you tell her then?" the other immortal asked.

"Well, my mother is over ninety years old and practically blind from glaucoma and macular degeneration, so I don't think I need to worry about her noticing any changes," Ernest replied. "She needs someone to care for her, and I am that person."

"Besides," the first vampire insisted, "an informant tells us you are keeping a sort of chronicle, some kind of journal about our history."

"Yeah, but it has nothing about what you are seeking. It's just about my personal observations, not about events I didn't witness," Ernest said, defending himself.

The second immortal, who seemed to be in charge, said, "I am going to search every inch of this place and all your papers."

Earnest grasped at straws and said, "Don't you need a search warrant for that?"

Immediately, both vampires burst into laughter. "Who do you think we are, the police?" the first immortal said.

VI. NIGHT COURT

"Kneel scum, before His Majesty, Archaelogos II, He Whose Name No Mortal May Speak, King of all Vampires." Two powerful immortals forced Ernest to his knees although he would have knelt voluntarily if they had allowed him.

Earnest was terrified; he had spent the previous two days in a dungeon without a drop of blood. Now he was in the middle of a huge chamber. A great well-lit chandelier hung above it, and elegantly dressed vampires were standing along its walls. Two other guards forced Harold to his knees, and Ernest saw that his face registered fear and anger. What justice could he expect from a vampire king?

Archaelogos looked down from his throne which rose on a dais, so high his feet were at the level of a man's head. His remote figure was grim but powerful, a simple gold circlet crowned his brows, and beneath his royal cloak of imperial purple was a man of steel with a mind and body at the peak of vampiric power. In his right hand was not a golden scepter but an axe of burnished steel. Four vampires armed with drawn swords stood sentry, one at each corner of the platform, like so many statues.

Then the black-clad vampire accuser stepped forward with a bow. "Your Majesty, your predecessor sent us out to find out what became of Clarissa Santiago's child. We discovered that this newbie, Ernest Frank, spared by your predecessor, had been keeping a chronicle that endangers all vampires. For this he should die, staked and exposed under the sun. It appears that Harold called Halbmann is in fact the son of the executed woman. Now is the time to end their miserable existence."

The King directed his stony gaze at the prosecutor. "I have had read the Koine translation of his chronicle, and except that it is in English, I find no fault with it. Mortals must not be allowed to read it. It must be changed into Greek or Latin at once and the original copy destroyed. We do not want anything written in vernacular tongues," declared the King.

When he heard this, Ernest was tempted to protest that English—real English, not the neo-English or Newspeak that passes for it—is already a dead language, lost to all but the few still living born before 1960. He decided, however, it was safer to keep silent.

"We are ready," resumed the prosecutor, "to destroy Harold, to stake him and expose him under the sun at your orders. You have already read our report on all his deeds."

"Why should we do that?" the King asked. "Harold has a shown willingness to act behind the scenes, revealing nothing to mortal eyes, and has demonstrated almost a total lack of ambition for power. What harm has he done to immortals or to me? Restore to him his name Santiago and his grandfather's title Eternal Guardian of the Southern Realm, for he has certainly proved himself that already. There was some justification for the previous King's acts against Richard York and Sam Santiago, but the execution of Clarissa, Emily, and John Strange strikes us as excessive and cruel. The staking out of the nursing mother of a rare natural-born vampire, in particular, violates the traditions of our law."

"Surely these two must die," the prosecutor objected.

"Must is not a word to use to kings," said Archeologos, and he fixed his fierce gaze on the prosecutor. "Your cases are dismissed."

Then Ernest thought to himself, *Vengeance is mine, saith the Lord. Truly God's justice catches up even to kings, and his mercy toward sinners is amazing. There was justice in this vampire world, at least in this case. Now Harold could flourish without fear, and he would be a protection to all those of his house and many others besides.*

WINTER IN LAS VEGAS

I. THE NEW VEGAS

At twilight, Harold got in his car to go to his auto dealership, Halbmann Motors, one of his several businesses. He set his destination into the navigation system, started the car, and backed down his driveway into the street. Elsewhere, he knew his car would appear as a blip on the control system, which took over his car, and drove it over the invisible railroad to his office. He relaxed and considered taking a short nap during the journey. Of course, he engaged his collision avoidance system, but really, that was unnecessary because every car on the street was on the navigation grid, which was guiding them all to their destination the shortest and best way. Nowadays, people needed a driver's license only if they were driving in rural areas where the net did not yet extend.

Harold thought about how different the Las Vegas was since his youth. Growth had virtually stopped, and in fact, the outermost bands of suburban development lay abandoned in most cases, worthless without water lines since in those districts, they were also abandoned. In some areas, fires had left only vacant concrete pads where houses had stood and charred wood half covered by drifting sand. Other houses stood abandoned on the streets, neglected buildings with sagging roofs and fading paint, yards overgrown by desert plants that were again taking hold. Grass sprang up from the cracked pavement of unused roads. Coyotes wandered along them and approached closer to the city, seeking a stray dog or cat to supplement a diet of rabbits or the occasional feral burro. Sure, the valley still had nearly five hundred thousand residents, but gaming was now legal everywhere, and there were casinos in every single State in the United States and not just among a few Native American tribes. Las Vegas got its water from wells and the third straw from Lake Mead as the other two were high and dry. The bathtub ring around the lake was an immense band of white. Ironically, many miles of water pipe ran northward, connecting Las Vegas with nowhere. In its wisdom, the US Supreme Court had ruled that the city, no matter the number its of inhabitants, had no right to despoil the native peoples, the ranchers or communities of northern Nevada, or even the natural environments of their precious water. Millions that could have been put into building a plant in California to get water from the sea had gone instead to build a useless aqueduct.

This November, the few oak, maple, or fruit trees in the suburban neighborhood had been gradually losing their leaves, which were painted in dark reds, browns, or yellow. Fall in Las Vegas was never as spectacular as in communities where frost touched the trees early and transformed their leaves into brilliant hues. Some trees still had a few green leaves at the start of December.

West of the city, the mountains of the Spring Range, immense jagged blocks of gray and brown stone speckled with desert vegetation rose into the overcast sky. The lowering clouds contributed only a desultory sprinkle of rain drops. Higher in the mountains, Harold knew there would be showers, and by the early morning hours, a little snow. Soon, Mount Charleston would be finally covered with a snow cap that would last at least until June, when the melting snows on the mountain would spill down the rocky watercourses only to disappear and recharge the aquifer beneath the valley, source of the famous springs that had brought the first inhabitants so long ago. The mountains to the northeast were lower and seldom covered by winter snows.

Harold also noted the new trend in housing—virtual residences. Nowadays homeowners could have any kind of house they wished with the flip of a switch. For a few hundred dollars, an owner could surround his building with a hologram suggesting a medieval castle, a southern plantation house, a rustic rural lodge, any kind of structure one might wish. In fact, Harold recalled, when the new houses first appeared, a few con men had actually tried to sell gullible buyers hologram residences that had no structure within at all. Now smart buyers insisted that sellers turn off the machinery so they could make sure that the house within was real, weather-tight, and sound throughout. Okay, here we are at work, he observed, as the car slid smoothly into its parking space hands free.

II. AN IMPORTANT VISIT

While Harold was using the latest technology Ernest Hauptmann, once Ernest Frank, was doing something very different, using centuries old methods. He dipped his pen into the ink well and began writing on the page, the point moving smoothly over the parchment:

Hic incipit capitulum V, historia Haroldi Semiviri Protectoris Perpetui...

"Here begins chapter 5, the history of Harold Halbmann, Eternal Protector..."

Ernest looked at the text he was making and was pleased at its appearance. Officially, of course, Frank was dead, and his ashes were in an urn, in a niche, in a mausoleum in the southern part of town. Once his mother died, it seemed better to him to change identities so as not to have to explain his long life and relative youth. Right now, any observer would call him a man in his middle twenties.

After completing the page, Ernest put it up to dry and decided to take a break. He turned on the evening news. President Mikko Yamaguchi was going to visit Las Vegas again after her 2032 election campaign, it seemed. After the news, there was *Las Vegas View*, when two real estate developers were arguing over the new hologram homes. Ronald Snark, president of Bristlecone Realty, was unhappy with the new houses.

"Who in his right mind," he said, "would want a house that is nothing but an illusion? I mean, you can walk right through the walls as if they are not there. They are completely phony, and the valley is full of fine, existing homes that can be had for very reasonable money."

Justin Withers, President of Hologram Homes (Your house is your castle or anything else you want!) did not share this opinion. "These fine, existing homes, naturally, they are built of bricks and mortar or of wood with regular siding. And inside the interior walls are lath and plaster. Right?"

"No one had built a house like that for years," said Ronald. "They are mostly made of cement stucco on wire, over insulation, and the interior walls are constructed of gypsum dry-wall board."

"And, Mr. Snark, the doors are made with fine-paneled wood, the twelve light windows with individual panes of glass set in mullions. The floors are hardwood, maybe even parquet. True?"

"Certainly not. The doors are plastic, and the windows, single sheets of glass with a grid over them. The floors have rugs over the concrete slab. What's your point anyway?"

"Really, aren't your fine homes mostly illusion anyway. Everything is fake to keep the costs down, right? Even the tile roof is made of cement tile, not ceramic. As for the furnishings, they are made of pressed wood from sawmill shavings. So aren't hologram homes just a cheaper form of illusion? Anyway, if the hologram is set correctly, the walls stand so close to the interior structure that a visitor reaching out to touch it will always encounter the real wall beneath and never even know that the outer wall is fake. And these real homes of yours—how many are really connected anymore to water and services?"

Enough of that, Ernest thought. He switched off the television and went back to his work area, placed a fresh page on his *scriptorium*, dipped his pen back into the ink and began again. A few pages more, and it soon would be time to find someone to provide him his evening meal, and at that thought, his fangs descended and then retracted.

Later, Harold left his office and headed for the Golden Cornucopia, now dressed up as a Spanish castle. Hologram generators sure beat the expense of pulling down and constructing new buildings, he reflected. Tonight, there was fresh excitement among Richard Smith's crew. The President of the United States was swinging by on a post-election visit, and would be staying in the casino. Already Secret Service Agents, the *castrati*, were swarming all over the hotel and city looking for potential threats. Investigating the employees would be easy; most lived in the hotel. The new automobile registration laws taxed people based on how far they drove to work; there were plenty of rooms, and Richard likes to have his workers close to their jobs. So everyone was happy. The workers, fewer that there used to be, lived close to work, paid minimal costs to register their cars (if they had any), and there were still enough rooms for all visitors. Harold would have to be extra careful on the hunt, he thought. He didn't want to sink his fangs into some female agent or a *castratus*!

III. DISASTER PREPARATIONS

Afterwards, on his way to retrieve his auto parked in the garage under the Golden Cornucopia, Harold heard a terrific racket and looked over to see a crew drilling a hole into one of the massive concrete pillars under the hotel. Two guys in gray coveralls marked by a logo, were at work. The truck parked nearby carried a larger version of the logo, Irwin Engineers. People were always doing some kind of work in the casino, Harold knew, but he wondered just what all this noise was about. So he walked over.

"What are you doing?" Harold asked one of the men in an interval in their work.

"We're installing earthquake stress and vibration sensors," he replied. "They will detect any movement in the structure should there be tremors of any magnitude."

"Thanks," Harold said. "That's interesting to know." Then he headed back to his vehicle, his curiosity satisfied.

When Harold returned to his apartment, well satisfied with the local blonde who had fed him a delicious meal, he turned on the television to catch the news. *News Now* reported that the President would visit again on Thursday, naturally without any reference to just where she would be staying. She would be attending a dinner for wealthy donors held at the Palace Hotel, visiting with democratic leaders, then flying back to Washington.

Maria Gonzalez, the woman news anchor, noted, "And, of course, she will be accompanied by the famous Secret Service protection detail, the *castrati*."

"Yeah," Ed Richardson observed. "They were nicknamed that after the President reformed them to make sure half were women, and the rest would have no longer interested in recreational sex. I just wonder how any guy would agree to be castrated no matter how great the pay and benefits. Wouldn't their wives object?"

"It's not that much of a problem," said Maria, "since they remove the sperm and freeze it at the time of the castration, so the men can have children whenever they want. They just have to give up sex for fun."

"Well, I suppose that's one way to keep down scandals," Ed said, "but it seems pretty extreme to me."

What a mess, Harold thought, and he turned off the television. Now these guys and the women were all over town mingling with the natives and visitors. What would happen if a vampire happened to feed from one of them? It was a potential disaster waiting to happen.

❦

Two weeks earlier, in room 144 of Motel 20, George Swainston, Gloria Allred, Mike Jones, and Samuel Wright were in a meeting of their own.

"Look," said Mike, "the thing is to bring off this business as a one, two punch that will finish Las Vegas forever. The timing is critical. The first blow will distract the authorities' attention totally from the second one—the one that will end this blot on the landscape forever. It will be years, though, maybe centuries before the site will return to the natural state it had before Anglo-American settlers moved into the valley. I think the river will clean up a lot sooner."

Gloria was concerned about something else. "I understand the need to get rid of that Jap president who is just a tool for big business, but when we blow the dam, we could kill innocent people down river, even women and children."

"Not a problem," Mike said, "because as soon as we blow up Hoover Dam, I will call the police at Laughlin and warn them the dam has blown, so they can evacuate the zone down river. They will have just enough time if they believe me. If they don't, well then, it's their fault. What do you think, George?"

"I am sure there will be enough time before it reaches Laughlin to complete the evacuation. We are not trying to kill people, to terrorize. We are only trying to restore the natural balances destroyed by human greed, and to remove those office holders are who are supporting this destruction. Those who bought their offices from the great corporations that are destroying our world. Killing a few is unavoidable. Is everything ready, then?"

"It all set," Mike said. "And the no fly zone should not be a problem as far out as Lake Mead.

"Let's review the technical side of our preparations. We are drilling two holes in each pier or column in the parking garage under the Cornucopia, one on the top left side and one on bottom right. When we blow the charges, each column will fall on its right side. A single column falling would have little effect, but when we blow them all, we will bring down the house, literally speaking.

"Our C-47 will take off from the old abandoned Tonapah Army Airfield, built in the World War II, and Sam will pilot it remotely to Lake Mead, crash it into the lake right behind Hoover Dam. It may hit the dam or not, but when it reaches the right depth, a pressure detonator will blow up the explosives in it, and the shock wave will breach the dam, releasing a torrent that will sweep the river clean, destroying every manmade structure in its path."

Sam observed, "I'm sure you all agree I'm the Wright pilot to guide your C-47 to the target."

Upon hearing this terrible pun, Gloria and the rest of the group groaned audibly. They were able to conclude the meeting quickly right afterwards.

On his next visit, Harold found the engineers still at it drilling another immense column in the parking garage. They were as noisy as ever, and while Harold understood that they had things to do around the casino, he was just a little irritated by all the racket.

He saw the manager near the reception desk, so he asked him, "When are the engineers going to be finished with installing the earthquake monitoring system?"

"What earthquake monitoring system? I haven't heard a thing about it."

"Well, if you went down to your garage, you sure would. The noise is incredible."

"Let me call facilities. I'm sure they'll know what's going on down there." He picked up the phone and called his manager there, but the answering machine told him the man was out to dinner and would be back shortly.

"The manager is out right now, but I'm sure it must be okay," the manager said.

The next evening, the conspirators were again at Motel 20 hammering out the last-minute details of their plan, which they had set in motion. "It will really be spectacular when we bring down the casino," Mike said. "The whole building will collapse just as if in an implosion when we blow the charges right in the middle of the President's press conference. We will get her, half her cabinet and 2,500 or so guests. It will rival 9-11, and nobody, *nobody* will realize that another heavier blow will fall in minutes, destroying the dam and the city. Las Vegas will be history and we will all be famous. What do you think about it, Gloria?" he said as he observed a doubtful expression on her face.

"I think that a lot of perfectly innocent people will die. I know that operations such as this one always involve so called collateral damage, but I wish we could accomplish our purpose with less rather than more loss of life. It will be bad enough when that wall of water washes down the Colorado sweeping away everything in its path, but so many will die at the hotel too. Still, we are at war with those people and things like this happen in war-time. But is there anything we can do without arousing suspicion? Maybe we could start a rumor that the hotel has a bed-bug infestation or something that would make more people cancel at the last moment? What do you think, George?"

"Last minute changes like that could arouse suspicion that we don't want to create. When we bombed cities in Europe during World War II, do you think we told civilians when we were going to be dropping bombs or even warned them to get out of town? No, we simply struck and killed millions. That's just war."

"Let's hope the results justify resorting to this kind of mass murder," she said. "If we can eliminate this useless city that sucks the Colorado dry and pollutes the environment, if we can free the wild river and protect the endangered animal and plant species, and if we can destroy the foundations of our corrupt government, it will all be worthwhile."

A murmur of assent ran around the room as the conspirators turned to more mundane details, the timing of the operation, and coordination between the two attacks.

The phone on the hotel manager's desk was ringing. "Richard," the voice said, "this is Dan over in facilities returning your call. I believe you had a question?"

"Yeah, are Irwin Engineers installing an earthquake monitoring system right now? People are complaining about the racket from their drilling."

"Yes, that's right, but they're not supposed to start until next month," Dan said. "Generally, it's great when a contractor starts early, but having all that racket just as we're making final preparations for a presidential visit is distracting. I'll give them a call first thing in the morning and ask them to back off for a few days until the visit is over."

IV. A Romance Begins

Harold went to the Golden Cornucopia just a couple of hours later. He thought the girl at the bar was one of the most beautiful he had seen. She was raven haired with arresting eyes, delicate features and was five feet six, slender with nice breasts and curves. She was obviously dressed for a night of clubbing in a black velvet minidress that showed much of her breasts and her great legs. Although he was looking for a meal at the time, Harold thought this girl could be a keeper, someone worth a long-term relationship, though he doubted that the girl would have any idea of what that might mean considering he was a vampire.

Taking advantage of an open space next to the girl at the bar, Harold ordered a martini and then looked around at his attractive neighbor.

"Come to Las Vegas often?" he said, opening the conversation.

"I travel a lot," she said, "but seldom to Las Vegas."

"Well, I don't think any city can beat the night life here. The clubs are all smoking," he said. "Oh, by the way, I am Harold Halbmann. And you are?"

"Cindy Craftsman. Where are you from?" she asked.

"Actually, I come from Las Vegas and know the city very well. I could suggest clubs here that would be a lot of fun, if you would like. And where to you come from?"

"I come from the Washington, DC, area and live in Fairfax, Virginia, just outside the district. I work for a lobbyist for defense contractors there and thought it would be fun to come to Vegas. What do you do?" she asked with an appreciative glance.

"Actually, I own several businesses around town, the most well-known being Halbmann Motors. Nothing very exciting, I'm afraid, but they bring in the bucks. Some of our best night spots are Flames of Love, American Girl, the Bordello Club, Rock the Night. I'd love to show you the town."

"That might be fun. I could meet up with you over there after dinner."

"Sounds good, but maybe we could have dinner here first and get to know each over a little better. This casino has all kinds of restaurants—Chinese, Japanese, and French. Take your choice."

They decided on dinner at the Great Wall, a Chinese restaurant. After they sat down to an excellent dinner, they resumed their conversation in earnest.

"What was it like growing up in Washington?" Harold wanted to know.

"We usually refer to it as DC," Cindy replied, "to distinguish it from Washington State. Actually, my family didn't move there until I was six. My dad worked for the government and was assigned over at the Pentagon then. I loved the city with its parks, monuments, and museums, and everything. I studied art in a course offered by the Corcoran Art Museum, even, but I never became another Picasso. It was fun, though, horseback riding on weekends, visiting Great Falls in the summer and riding on its merry go round, seeing the old canals, and all of that. I studied at American University there also, and in the summer, I used to hike over to the National Cathedral, this fantastic Gothic church. Did you grow up in Las Vegas?"

"I'm one of a very few who did. Tell about your family."

"Well, I have an older brother who lives in Baltimore and a sister who lives in Saint Louis, Missouri. We're not too close, but we usually get together a couple of times a year. How about your folks?"

"Well, I was orphaned at an early age and raised near here by an aunt. I went to high school in Vegas and attended the Community College. It's an interesting place to grow up. It was hard, and I'm sure very different."

When they descended into the parking garage beneath the casino, Harold noticed that one of the Irwin Engineers trucks was still parked there and that various scaffolding was around some of the concrete piers that supported the hotel.

"You should have been here this afternoon," he told Cindy. "The din was incredible. They are installing some kind of earthquake monitoring system. When I asked about it even the manager, seemed to know nothing about it, he had to call facilities. I hope they get this thing wrapped up soon."

"Really, that's interesting," Cindy said. "I suppose it will measure the movement of the structure in the event of an earthquake."

"Well, Cindy, Vegas is not California and earthquakes here are rare, although not unknown, but I suppose it's better to be prepared and learn from them than not. Still, I'm surprised that they are doing that considering that it must be expensive."

They spent a great night at the Flames of Love, still a vampire-operated club where a few very observant persons might have noticed that none of the staff seemed never to age much.

After a several dances, Cindy excused herself and headed toward the rest room. She took out her cell and phoned her superior. "Sam, I'm wondering about some work Irwin Engineers is doing under the casino, installing an earthquake monitoring system. There're probably legitimate, but you can't be too safe."

"I'm glad you're so careful," Sam replied, "but we've already checked on it. Irwin is a legitimate company scheduled to do that work. They seem just a little ahead of schedule, that's all. Just enjoy the town. After all, you are supposed to be off duty now."

Cindy invited Harold to her room after the dancing. They sat on a sofa just inside the door kissing and caressing.

"I want you to know I really wish we had more time," she said, coming up for air. "This job of mine just doesn't let me get to know people gradually, but you're just too smoking for me to pass up."

"I really want to love you not for only a night, but right now, maybe we should move into the bedroom.

They went in sat down together on the edge of the bed and their hands got busy. Cindy removed her dress, and he his shirt and pants. Then they were kissing again, and he reached around to release her bra, so he could kiss the nipples of her breasts. Harold's hands were all over her body stroking while they kissed. At last she stood up so he could remove her panties, and then, they were on the bed his fingers touching her intimately. Her face and breasts were already flushed when she opened her legs, so he might enter. He plunged into her, driving, driving, and then, his fangs pierced her neck the moment before he exploded. He drank but little, and his kisses healed the wounds that would have marked her neck. At last, they were exhausted, and she cuddled against him, and they lay together, his hand around her and her head upon his right shoulder.

"Wow," he said, and she sighed in reply.

V. ROMANCE INTERRUPTED

Next morning, Harold got up early, and he left a note for Cindy, whom he did not awake. He wrote,

> It was wonderful. I want to see more of you if I may. Here are my address and phone number, should you have to leave town early. Anyway, I'll call you at six in the evening, in case you are in. Love (and I really mean it), Harold.

He went down stairs for a cup of coffee and realized it sucks to be a vampire in a world where everyone else wakes up with daylight and that just makes you drowsy. Truthfully, he had admitted to Cindy yesterday that he was a night person. After checking on his business, he would find some place for a nap after lunchtime and revive later in the afternoon.

Meanwhile, Irwin Engineering was returning its call from facilities asking for them to back off installation of its earthquake monitoring system.

"Dan," the manager said, "I don't understand what you are talking about. We don't have any trucks or people at the casino. And we will be placing our sensors on the piers, yes, but not drilling into them. It will not cause very much noise at all."

"Who can it be then? Who is over there?"

Dan picked up his telephone and called his boss, "Richard, I just talked with Irwin Engineering, and they say they haven't started work yet and that their work won't involve drilling the piers to install sensors. The sensors will go on the outside of the pillars instead. Something really weird is going on."

Richard thought maybe he should call security and have them investigate. Was this a scam of some kind? Maybe he should inform Mr. Samuel Smith, the CEO.

That afternoon, Harold returned to the Golden Cornucopia, determined to find someone to drink from before calling Cindy to see if she was free. It was better, safer, to feed first and then arrange for a date.

Irwin Engineers were still hard and work in the garage, and the noise was worse than ever, but they seem to have almost completed their task. It looked like there was only one row of the columns left to be completed. Still, it was really irritating.

Then Harold appeared at the manager's to complain. "They are still down there making the God-awful racket I was telling you about. How long is going to take before they finish?"

"I don't know what's going on," Dan said. "I was about to send some people from security later to see what the heck those people are doing, but things got too busy."

Suddenly, a cold chill ran through Harold. Maybe, just maybe, what these guys were doing was related to the presidential visit.

"I think you should investigate sooner rather than later," he said, and he walked out of the room.

High overhead, Air Force One approached the runway at Nellis AFB, just outside Las Vegas. Six AF-400 Bs, the escort of honor broke away and headed for their base at the nearby Creech AFB. Each of these fighters was only ten feet long with a twenty-foot wingspan. None of these airplanes had a cockpit. The pilots were teenagers with video game experience chosen for their fast reaction times, who were sitting behind a console at the base. Each fighter could carry two AIM-96B missiles under its wings. These heat-seeking missiles could bring down aircraft that were beyond eyesight, and the pilots could set them to lock on to any one particular kind of engine. Once locked on though, nothing would shake them, not climbing toward the sun nor diving down toward the heat radiating desert floor. When cloaking was engaged, the fighters could also simply disappear, visible only to aircraft with the same identification friend or foe system. Today, of course, they were entirely visible as they pulled away from the presidential aircraft. Down at the base below, a motorcade had assembled to escort the Chief Executive to the Golden Cornucopia.

Harold decided that he needed to look into what was going on personally. He descended to the garage and went to his car. He waited patiently for a half hour, and when he saw one of the workers headed for the rest room, which was some distance away, he waited until he reemerged then seized him by the collar and forced him back inside, pushed him against a wall next to the row of urinals.

"I want to know who put you up to this. Who are you, and just who is behind this? Tell me now or die!" He fixed his gaze on the unfortunate victim, and his fangs slid out.

"George...Arnold," he stammered. "Mike Jones...he...he said we would all be heroes and...and save the country...when... when we destroy this cesspool."

"You are going to blow up the casino? And while the President is here?"

"Mike told us that bitch should die for everyone's sake."

"What else aren't you telling me?" Harold could sense evasion.

"We're also going to blow the dam."

"Hoover Dam?"

"That's right."

"When?"

"Right after we...we...bring down the Cornucopia."

Harold tore into the man's throat with his fangs and drank deeply. But he didn't kill him, and instead, Harold erased his memory and sent him back to his job.

Then Harold took out his cellular and called Cindy.

"Cindy, this is Harold. I'm sorry we won't have time for a date tonight. You need to get out of the hotel—now! I've discovered a plot to blow it up. I'm on my way to hotel security right now."

"Harold, I just have to see you now. It's really important."

"Then meet me at hotel security!" Harold exclaimed. "But pack your bags first. You've got to get out of this hotel."

Harold arrived at the hotel security.

"You overheard two of the workers from Irwin Engineers talking about blowing up the hotel?" the hotel security man said. His face was incredulous. "Don't they have a contract for an earthquake monitoring system?"

"These guys are not really from Irwin Engineers," Harold said. "If you don't believe me, call the manager."

The security guard picked up the phone and called. The manager picked up and identified himself. "This is Ronald Richardson from security. A guy, Harold Halbmann, tells me that Irwin is not working in the hotel, right now."

"Yes," said the manager. "He's right. Someone must be working some kind of scam or something. We've been so busy with preparation for the visit that I haven't had a chance to contact you."

"Harold says they are planning to blow up the hotel."

"What! How does he know that?"

"He says he overheard them."

"Then call the police. But don't evacuate the hotel until we can confirm that information."

Ronald called the police and then turned to the two men in his office. "Max," Ronald said to his assistant, "come along with Mr. Halbmann and me. We are going to find out what this is all about."

At that moment, Cindy, dressed in a blouse and slacks and a tall thin man in a conservative blue suit and tie walked through the open door of the office.

"I am Agent Cindy Craftsman, Secret Service, and this is Agent George Zimmermann," she said. "We've heard something we need to investigate."

"We're going down right now to straighten out this business," Ronald said. "The police should be here soon too."

When they reached the parking garage, they walked toward the workmen. They saw six men working on one of the piers, one of whom glanced nervously at the security guards. The workers' truck marked Irwin Engineers was parked behind them.

"Who are you guys?" Ronald asked.

"We're from Irwin Engineering, working on the contract to install earthquake sensors," the foreman said.

"You sure are not Irwin Engineers," Ronald said. "So just who are you and what are you doing here?"

Six men drew their handguns out of their coveralls and opened a hot fire on the guards. Two others standing behind the truck could not engage.

Ronald had just cleared his holster with his semiautomatic when three bullets pierced him, and he fell to the ground. Max had actually fired one round that went wide when he was felled by a bullet.

George had his weapon out and fired a round at one of the conspirators, but his first shot missed, chipping one of the concrete piers and ricocheting across the garage.

Cindy had drawn her weapon and shot down one of the men, only to fall under a hail of bullets. Like the other agents, she had to use a semi-automatic. Agents could not use a recoilless machine pistol because they usually worked around crowds.

George hit the man with his second shot squarely in the chest, and then, he shifted his aim to a second man.

Harold, whom they had ignored up to this point, sprang forward and ripped open the jugular of one conspirator then hurled him into another who dropped his gun.

George took down his second enemy and shifted to a third but was struck and knocked down by bullets from that man and fell down hard on the concrete deck.

Meanwhile, Harold jumped on a third enemy and ripped open his throat, then whirled to attack another, but two bullets struck him, tearing through his chest but missing his heart.

With five of their number down and the likelihood of more security staff or police arriving soon, the remaining conspirators lost heart, piled into their truck, and took off. Blood was everywhere as were 9-mm cartridge cases scattered among the blood-spattered bodies. Two thirds of the charges to bring down the hotel had already been set; the others lay at the base of the piers, waiting to be inserted with their detonators.

Harold was on his feet in moments and immediately rushed to Cindy's side. It was bad, very bad. She had been hit twice in the chest and once in the thigh. Quickly, he slashed his arm with a pocket knife, opened her mouth with his fingers, and allowed a trickle of blood to fall into it. Both the guards and George were dead or unconscious. Then he picked Cindy up and put her onto the back seat of his car, then started up, and left the casino.

He set the navigation system for his home and turned his attention to Cindy. His own wounds still hurt, but he knew that they would heal fast. He had never ever turned anyone. Would it work? In theory, he knew how, but he had no practical experience. He was halfway home, and then, he stopped. He changed his destination to Aunt Julia's place. She would know how to help.

When he arrived, he picked up Cindy and carried her into Julia's cottage, then called her in from the brothel.

When Julia heard the news, she put an assistant in charge and came over at once. Harold told her what had happened and what he had done to save her.

"She'll have a chance," Julia opined, "but she'll have to accept her new state. She'll have to live with the fact that she'll become a vampire, and that she never had the choice of turning or not. It took a long while to reconcile your mother. Cindy may not like you much for turning her."

"She was dying. I didn't want her to die," Harold said. "I thought maybe she can be a partner to me in this world, a companion for the centuries to come."

Julia looked at him with sympathy because he had been through so much. He had lost his parents before he even knew them. She hoped with all her heart, her mind, and her soul that this girl could be the one for Harold. Only time would tell.

Julie called in two of the girls, Joyce and Elvira, she knew and trusted, to help see Cindy through the worst of the transformation and asked two maids to remain in her cottage afterword to provide nourishment. She sent Harold out of the room, promising to call him back as soon as Cindy opened her eyes.

Harold turned on the television to see what had happened. Had he effectively defeated the conspirators or not?

"In breaking news, a plot to kill our President has been foiled by quick thinking security guards at the Golden Cornucopia, who died heroes at the hands of conspirators. Presidential security agents also engaged the criminals in a wild battle. It appears that the conspirators kidnapped one female agent when they fled after their plan to blow up the Golden Cornucopia was discovered. Interrogation of two wounded conspirators revealed they also intended to blow up Hoover Dam. They raved they had been attacked by a demon. The President's party moved to a different hotel and plans for her address have been changed to the Thomas and Mac Center on Friday at 2:00 p.m. All the criminals' plans were frustrated thanks to an unknown individual who overhead the plotters talking and informed hotel security. Guests who had been evacuated returned to their rooms at the Golden Cornucopia, after officials confirmed that it was safe."

"Harold, come in now. She's awake," Julia said, and the young vampire hastened to the side of his beloved.

"What's...happening to me?" Cindy said. "I'm starving." She sat up as her eyes glowed, and new fangs descended for the first time, startling her. "Harold," she said, looking at him, "I didn't tell you who I am. I'm—"

"A former Secret Service Agent and a new vampire," Harold said, finishing her sentence. "You must eat now, and then, we can talk about your future."

Julia said, "I have asked Maria Saenz to help you with your first feeding. Remember Cindy you mustn't take too much. It could hurt her if you did."

Cindy plunged her fangs into Maria. Harold, Julia, and Elvira stood by since new vampires are often completely overcome by bloodlust.

After a few minutes Julia said, "That's enough." Harold and Elvira had stationed themselves where they could pull her back.

Cindy seemed to understand though and pulled back on her own. She was still ravenous, so she drank from Mercedes Menendez.

"Cindy," Harold said, "we need to talk. I'm sure Julia and our friends will understand that we have important things to discuss."

Harold seated himself close to Cindy and looked into her eyes, while the rest of the group left the room.

"Cindy, hear me out. We had just started to become intimate, but I already love you. I won't press you about this because so much has happened, too many changes to your life for you to adjust to it all. Now that you've become a vampire, almost everything has to change, not just your diet, but the whole rhythm of your days. You will need to learn how to feed off living men and women and leave them alive still. Your days are now your nights and your nights are your days. You won't be able to keep working at the same job. Julia has been through it all and can help."

Cindy seemed a little stunned at his words.

"I would wish, more than a million times, that you had chosen this life to be with me, to share long centuries that can become lonely for our kind. Normally, I wouldn't have done this to you until you had agreed you wanted to share my life, but I just had to save you. You're too wonderful a woman to die because of some scumbags."

Cindy fixed her eyes on Harold as it all soaked in.

"I know how hard it can be to take up the different life of an immortal. Julia and Ernest told me my own mother had a great deal of trouble adjusting. I hope you do, Cindy, and can be happy with the new centuries of life that are yours to enjoy. I also hope that you will choose to spend those centuries with me."

Cindy smiled at that.

"One problem you mentioned before is gone now. We have all the time in the world to really get to know each other. We'll take it slow now. No sex just yet. I'll court you as if we were living in another age. What do you say?"

"Well," said Cindy, with a twinkle in her eye, "the part about you courting me like in the old days sounds cool, but the no sex part stinks. Especially after that incredible night we spent together. It is going to be hard to adjust to all the changes, but I really want you to help me too, not just Julia."

VI. Love and Marriage, Vampire Style

Harold and Julia worked together to teach Cindy how to live as an immortal. They worked well as a team. Harold could teach her about hunting; Julia instructed her about how to be a female vampire, about intimate things—including conception, pregnancy, and child birth—and fun things too—hair and clothing styles favored by her kind.

Meanwhile, the end of the conspiracy was played out on national television. The news showed a sullen-looking Gloria Allred and a disheveled Samuel Wright being led away in handcuffs. Three of the conspirators had died in the shootout in the parking garage. Several had made their escape and were still at large. Charges of conspiracy to kill the President and murder for the deaths of the security guards and the presumed death of Cindy, as well as for her kidnapping were pending.

"They didn't really kidnap me," she objected to Harold, "nor kill me either."

Harold replied, "You were so close to death, I could barely raise your pulse, and you are, in fact, no longer living as a human. The kidnapping charge is a bit off, but it couldn't happen to more deserving people. I think those folks earned everything the prosecution can throw at them."

Harold and Julia continued instructing Cindy in the ways of immortals. Some things about the vampire state were very hard for Cindy to face. Her career was gone, and she could no longer visit with family members.

"Cindy," Harold said, "you will know more about your family as a vampire than you ever could as a mortal. You will know the children of their children, watch them prosper from afar, and sometimes, not always, you can intervene to help them without their even knowing it. We can destroy life, it is certainly true, but we can guard it also, both from rogues of our kind and from human criminals. This I have already learned in my short life as an immortal. Maybe you can't give your family members a hug anymore, but you can help them. What you lose is their appreciation of the fact. They must never know you still live."

Harold and Cindy would go clubbing on Friday nights and to the movies on Mondays or Wednesdays. He took her to Chinese and Mexican, French, and Italian restaurants to sample the cuisine.

"Now, Cindy," Harold explained, over a plate of delicious shrimp primavera, "we can enjoy this food almost as well as any human, but it will not sustain us long term. For that, we need blood, preferably human blood, although in a pinch animal blood will do. Regular human food is not enough, but we can still dine and drink wine with humans and socialize with friends."

"Wow, what a marvelous Las Vegas City is. The restaurants are wonderful! You are really spoiling me, Harold."

On Tuesdays and Thursdays, they dined in at Julia's place and watched videos or danced to the music of CDs or records. Then they would settle in on a sofa and begin to kiss and cuddle. She felt so alive when her man held her, and she opened her lips under his firm kisses. Their hands explored each other until each knew every inch of the other's body. Their excitement built under the caresses until they wound up in bed to complete their mutual enjoyment. Her cheeks and breasts blushed under his touch and kisses. They tasted each other. When she felt him thrust within her, she would have goosebumps, and she exploded repeatedly sometimes even before he came.

Then one Sunday afternoon, Harold knelt and offered her a box with a beautiful diamond and platinum ring. "Cindy," he asked, "would you marry me and share all the centuries and ages that will be mine?"

Cindy smiled at him and her eyes sparked with excitement.

"Yes," she replied. "Yes, now and forever."

Cindy decided to organize her own security business in Las Vegas, which might also include some private detective work. She could find others in the town's vampire community who she could employ to assist her own efforts. Her newfound powers as an immortal would only add to her effectiveness, she mused. She need work to engage her mind and her fierce energies, but even more, she needed something else, a part of Harold and a part of her, a new creation, and a sign that truly she and he had really become one flesh. It could take a century for her time for a child to come, and if so, she would wait, but maybe, just maybe, that first time, before she was a vampire, could have started more than just their love.

Winter expired with January, and the first blossoms on the fruit trees opened in mid- February as the time they had set for the wedding hastened on. Julia rented a hall at the Cornucopia. The women decorated it with festoons of white silk ribbon and garlands of oak and ivy. On one side, they placed an altar covered with a white cloth, and on it, they placed a plain cross and a chalice of fine silver. On that marvelous day, the entire vampire community gathered. All were there. Julia was there, of course, and Delia, especially since Harold was of her line, and another of hers had brought down a king and now reigned in his stead. Ernest and all the rest were there too.

Cindy was dressed in white, not as a symbol of her physical virginity, for a bump was clearly evident, but as a sign of her spiritual purity, and with a white veil, so that on that day, her new husband would be the first to look upon the beauty of her face, and around her head was a crown of spring flowers, symbol of her as an eternal hope for rebirth. Harold was dressed in a magnificent tuxedo, and around his head was a crown of laurel and oak leaves as a sign of his victories over every one of the enemies of his family and to mark that he was savior of his city and had rescued the ruler of his land. And on the day of his wedding, is not every man a king? Spring was in full glory on that day full of promise. The pastor had been ordained before a vampire turned him, and he refused to believe that any man might be dammed for another's deed. He told the people that marriage was a union blessed by God, and the requirements for a vampire marriage were the same as for humans, except longer.

"Do you, Harold, take this woman Cindy as your wife, in good times and bad, henceforth and forevermore?"

"I do."

"Do you, Cindy, take this man Harold as your husband, in good times and bad, henceforth and forevermore?

"I do."

"You may bestow the ring in token of your union.

"With this ring, I thee wed," Harold said, placing it on her finger, "and with all my goods, I thee endow."

"Where you are lord, I am lady," she replied.

Then he said, "Where you are lady, I am lord."

"Take then this cup in remembrance of Him, who shed his blood so that all, human or vampire, might have everlasting life."

Then Harold drank from the cup, and he passed it to Cindy, and thus they shared blood.

"By the authority of Almighty God, I pronounce you man and wife. You may kiss the bride."

Harold parted Cindy's veil and kissed her.

After the feast and on the next day, Ernest sat down at his *scriptorium* and placed a parchment before him, took a quill, trimmed it, and dipped its point into the ink, and began the last part of the chapter: *Die quinta Maii, Cinerella Haroldo nupsit, qui illam in matrimonium duxit.* "On the fifth of May, Cindy veiled herself for Harold, who married her."

His pen moved evenly, and the letters flowed perfectly, and at last, at the very end, confidently, he wrote: *Dies fugiunt, sed verbum scriptum manet.* "The days fly away, but the written word remains."

Throne of Blood—The Struggle for Absolute Power

I. Welcome, Richard

It was a beautiful Saturday morning in Las Vegas. There was not a single cloud in the sky. The rising sun painted the western ranges in gold. Harold and Cindy were celebrating the first birthday of their new son, Richard, and most of the vampire community had come to visit them in their house which stood high on the outskirts of Las Vegas. A beautiful home fitted with an array of solar panels and a wind generator, it stood proud and lonely over acres and acres of abandoned buildings, their paint flaking and some of the roofs sagging. Many old houses had been vandalized and stripped of their copper wiring by thieves. The streets, though, were mostly cracked but passable, except for some low places where too much gravel and debris had washed over them. Harold and Cindy got their water from a large cistern, which they could refill from a deep well. They had a septic system for sewage. There was no longer any electric, water, or sewer service in this abandoned district. The isolation was perfect, however, for bringing up a vampire child, who would need a lot of education before he could safely interact with humans. The couple had just seen off the last of their guests an hour before and were settling into bed at first light.

Harold, son a former Nevada Governor, in fact its first and only vampire governor, was Eternal Protector of the South, a title some said inherited, but all knew it was really well earned. Harold had a wide face, black hair, brown eyes, and very regular features, with just a suggestion of stubble over his jaw. He stood just a little taller than Cindy, the beautiful woman beside him with an oblong face, green eyes, and dark hair falling to her shoulder. Harold was hoping Richard would not inherit his dyslexia, but he was happy because he knew he could count on his Uncle Frank and Aunt Julia to assist him in the difficult task of educating his son. He, himself, as a child, had been constantly restless and unable to concentrate on reading. He could read fairly well now, but it was never a pleasure. He found his joy in other things, all kinds of music, cooking good food (Yes, vampires can enjoy food too; it's just not enough alone to sustain them). He loved to dance with his wife, Cindy, to hunt, to ride horseback, and to practice with his weapons, firearms, bows, and swords. Skill with arms had more than once saved his life and those of his friends.

The party had begun about ten o'clock Friday evening. Half an hour later, it was well underway. Already seated on the comfortable couch beneath the window were Aunt Julia Strange, the slender former show girl, with the kind eyes, who towered over Uncle Ernest Frank, seated beside her. Ernest's rectangular face, framed by large ears and his blond hair, had rather a high forehead, his jaw tapered to a somewhat square chin, his nose was prominent but straight, and two blue eyes looked out from beneath his craggy brows. He spoke, read, and wrote three languages well—including Latin—and knew something of two more. He kept a chronicle of vampire history secretly, hidden from most men.

Delia, a beautiful blonde, with curves in all the right places, stood talking to Harold and his wife. An important hostess on the club scene, this woman who seemed to be perhaps twenty-five was by far the oldest person in the house and even in Las Vegas. But then, she was an immortal like the majority of the guests, and because of her connections, she wielded considerable power.

The doorbell rang, and Harold walked over and opened it. There stood Ronald Andrews, Satrap of Nevada, two hundred and sixty pounds, six foot two, a vampire massive as he was mighty. Somewhat formally dressed in a gray silk suit and striped tie, he extended his hand toward Harold.

"Welcome, sir," Harold said.

They clasped hands briefly, and the Satrap remarked, "It's great to celebrate this day with you both. A true born immortal child is a rare thing, and now that he has survived his first year, I am sure that very soon he will bring fame and renown to your house."

"Thank you, sir," Harold said.

"Unfortunately, my wife Genevieve couldn't make it today due to a long-standing commitment. These two are my guards and confidants, Jerry Richardson and Harry Reeves," he said, gesturing toward the two large vampires escorting him.

"Welcome to you also," Harold observed.

One of the guards placed a gift for Harold's new son on the coffee table; from the shape of the package, Harold guessed that it might be a miniature sword, a not inappropriate gift for a new male vampire.

Harold and Cindy's guests included some of the beautiful girls from Aunt Julia's brothel, who were demurely dressed, plus other men and women from Las Vegas's immortal night club scene and the hotels. Dave Brubeck's jazz music played in the background, while the guests conversed among themselves, quaffed wine glasses filled with warm bottled blood, or drank from some humans who really wanted to meet a vampire. Harold had taken care that none of these guests from the night clubs would suffer real harm, and they would be mesmerized so they only would recall they had a good time, but wouldn't remember any details.

Cindy was talking to Delia about her pregnancy and the birth of Richard; being a new mother of a vampire was quite an experience.

"Harold was afraid for me," Cindy observed, "because he had heard what a difficult time his own mother had with him. Fortunately, I was turned before I was far along in my pregnancy, and my body just seemed to adjust to the change. I didn't suffer the way Clarissa did. I just had a little of the usual morning sickness, and then began to gain weight. Then the time drew close, and suddenly my water broke. When I went into labor, it seemed like forever before he came out."

"It's always difficult for a mortal woman to bear an immortal's child," Delia said. "It is best when she is turned early, allowing for her body to adjust easier. Birth can be very painful and protracted otherwise. Often the child will not live. Your son made it through the first year; he should do just fine."

"Julia was really a great help," Cindy said. "I don't know what I would have done when my milk came in pink from my blood had she not told me what to expect. When Harold turned me, I had no idea my breasts would secrete some of my own blood along with my milk."

When it was time, Harold brought in Richard. He raised up his child before the assembled community.

"Behold Richard, son of Harold and Cindy." He beamed with pride.

"Welcome, Richard! Eternal life and victory over all of your enemies," the guests chorused in a centuries old ritual.

After a sumptuous feast, the guests stole away one by one most well aware of the approach of the rising sun. The humans were driven off to their hotels, after Harold made sure they would be unable to recall the route they had travelled. Then Harold and Cindy prepared for bed. Not that they couldn't have stayed up past dawn, but it was more comfortable to sleep in the day time, for the pair of them to lie side by side in bed spooning with Harold's right arm over his love. Soon, they would seem dead to the world, breathing and heartbeat undetectable.

That Monday, Harold returned to his desk. He was head of Halbmann Enterprises consisting of a half-dozen business, including Halbmann Motors, which sold automobiles specially modified with the new electrical, navigation, and fuel systems.

Halbmann Motors was very successful; thanks to the extension of the virtual railroad, a driver could go to any place in Las Vegas, and to some other cities in Nevada without touching the wheel of his car. He just had to program in his destination, technology, including a collision avoidance system, did the rest. The cars burned a non-polluting fuel, and a large solar panel built into the roof of each vehicle kept the battery from ever going flat. You could leave one of the cars parked for a decade, and it would still start the first time. Sales were good.

Harold had got up from a good nap after lunch. His office was cave-like. There were no windows at all; instead, it was illuminated by soft florescent lights. There was a leather covered sofa along one side of the room. A picture of his father's inauguration as governor, with his left hand on a Bible and his right raised, palm to the front, standing before the crowd hung on one wall along with a couple of shots of Harold fencing, one of him holding up the head of a buck he had shot. There were several photographs of his grandfather Big Richard Smith, founder of the Golden Cornucopia Casino, and of his mother, Clarissa, who had died soon after he was born. On the fine Persian carpet, his desk stood huge and held many things that recalled his life, school trophies, a paper weight from Big Richard's hotel, as well as his laptop, neatly folded up in the center.

His telephone rang, for Harold had an old-fashioned land line along with a cellular phone. He liked the privacy of talking over the wire instead of having every conversation broadcast to the whole world. He also much preferred the jingling of a telephone bell to the buzzing sounds or canned music of many phones. He turned around in his leather swivel chair and picked up his telephone receiver.

"Harold speaking...Yes, sir," he said. It was the Satrap who called. "I heard on television about the two visitors found drained of blood behind the hotel...Of course, sir, I don't want bad publicity for my relative's hotel, nor do I want the public to become suspicious about vampires here. This has to be some stranger from out of town who just doesn't care that he is drawing attention to his own kind. I'll help hunt him down, and if I catch him, I'll turn him over to you for trial and staking. If he's smart, he'll already be long gone by this time. He won't escape for long, no matter where he goes. The immortals there will find him and stake him for violating our prime directive, if for nothing else. I'll give you a call when I learn anything."

All immortals, Harold thought, *knew there were a few situations where it was very hard for a vampire to not to kill a human for his blood. For example, if an immortal had been trapped somewhere for centuries and were suddenly disturbed, the bloodlust could be irresistible. Or someone newly turned without proper supervision might completely drain a human. Aside from such emergencies, however, no intelligent vampire wanted to draw human attention to his existence by killing, when it was so easy to simply feed off an individual and then make him forget, or better yet, leave the person with a vague sensation of pleasure, that would make it easier to feed from him in the future. Only idiots sewed destruction far and wide; those idiots did not survive long as vampires.* Harold realized *that he would need to give some extra time to the club scene to investigate who might be responsible for these crimes.*

Dusk found him at the Flames of Love Night Club where he visited with Delia, in her small office, trying to better understand, who might be responsible for these random killings. Delia was just as concerned as the Satrap.

"The two bodies had been thrown into the Dumpster behind the club last week, and yesterday, two of our people found another pair right in the alley, also with all the marks of a vampire attack. They were drained, and their identification and money still with the bodies. I think this must be an attempt to expose and discredit us and our club scene," Delia observed.

"Our cleanup crew disposed of the remains in the desert."

"Who were the victims?" Harold asked. "Is there any indication as to why they were targeted?"

"The first two were Ralph Jones and Emily Patterson, but you probably already remember them from the news. The second were Elmer Johnson and Maria Osvaldo."

"Maybe it was an immortal pair then, a man and a woman. Otherwise, the choice of victims seems strange," Harold observed.

"They might just be trying to throw us off," Delia speculated. "I've asked all of my people here at the clubs, and no one has noticed anything strange or any vampires from out of the city. Obviously someone, some vampire or vampires from the outside, is working the clubs here, and he or she doesn't care about drawing suspicion down on us."

"Our Satrap has asked me to investigate these killings," Harold noted, "so I'm going to be prowling around your clubs looking for these criminals. Don't say anything to the staff, just in case anyone might be involved with the killers."

Later that evening, after he and his wife had fed, Harold and Cindy were together again at home, and Harold decided to raise the question with her.

"Cindy," he said, "You told me once you wanted to go into private investigations now that your government career is over. I wonder would you consider helping me track down the renegade vampires that are publicly slaughtering people in our night clubs. The Satrap has asked for my help, and now, I need yours."

"Of course, darling. It sounds very interesting, and now that our child is already a year old, it's time I started building a career for myself again."

"There're some things I need to teach you first, for your own safety, my dearest. I know you have had law-enforcement training including practice with weapons, but you have never faced immortal enemies before. The powerful machine pistols or the semiautomatic handguns that are still legal to own and can flatten any human are almost useless against our kind.

"The only sure ways to kill a vampire in combat are a direct shot to the heart or by severing the head from the body or else entirely destroying it. We can be burned up also, of course, but unless we are trapped, we generally spring out of any fire before we die. We can be killed by staking us out in the sun, but that is more of an execution than a combat.

"That means a shot aimed at the heart that misses by millimeters is a miss, and of no value. Almost severing a head is also useless, as are partial burns, since we heal with amazing speed. Silver can weaken us, but even a silver bullet won't kill unless it passed directly through the chambers of the heart.

"The broadsword and the crossbow are usually the most effective weapons, but they are rather too obvious. You, my sweet, are a weapon yourself and will be able to rip the throat out of any mortal man in the blink of an eye but will find your match and more than your match in an older immortal. So I will teach you how to use the traditional weapons.

"We must be cautious and crafty when we find the renegades. We will try to make sure they do not know we are hunting them. We will be just two more vampires out for the evening in quest of our dinners. We will avoid ambushes until we lay our own."

"How can we recognize them and be sure that they are the killers?" Cindy asked.

"We are looking for one or two immortals who are probably not from around here. I think, from their choice of victims, one male and one female each time, they might be a couple, but I could be wrong. They obviously have not the slightest respect for humans, and they are willing to ignore even our prime directive. We must observe them carefully without their knowing, and we will have some help from the casino's security cameras. Immortals give themselves away by little things, standing stock still too long, gazing without blinking, and by the occasional flash of the eyes when looking at a sexy person. We can learn to fake it, blinking from time to time, and hiding our feelings, but no one can cover every characteristic all of the time; sooner or later we give ourselves away.

"Wait a minute, and I will show you our weapons."

Harold disappeared into the back of the house and came back holding a long bag with a sling, and in the other hand, a crossbow and quiver with several quarrels. First, Harold showed Cindy how to aim the bow under the target at short range, directly at it at medium distance and to hold it high at longer range. He made her experiment until she got the feel of the bow and how it would shoot.

"Good shooting!" said Harold when one of Cindy's bolts pierced the center of the target. "The crossbow is very effective at night because we have such good night vision, and it never makes a muzzle flash the way firearms do. With a bit more practice, you'll be really deadly."

"Wow, that was fun really, but I hope I never really need to kill anyone."

"Now, my love, let's look at the sword, the main weapon for close combat."

Harold took the bag from the wall where he had stood it earlier, opened the zipper, and took out a pair of sabers. These were heavier than modern fencing sabers, with blades over three quarters of an inch wide near the hilt tapering toward the tip. The blade was straight, the guard wide enough to protect the knuckles, with a single heavy strap that connected to the pommel. He handed one to Cindy and showed her how to hold it.

"That groove on the back of the grip is for your thumb. The thumb directs the blade so in must go on top and not around the grip. There, this way." He showed her how to grasp the weapon.

"Great, that's the way! Now, the stance. Stand with your right foot advanced and forming a ninety-degree angle to your left, now bend your knees, and sink down slightly. Splendid, perfect. Now, to advance, step forward a short step with your front foot, then bring up your rear. The retreat is the same way, but backwards."

Harold showed Cindy the basic parries or defensive moves and showed her how they formed a sequence, from first, on the left, made when you clear the blade from its scabbard, edge left, second, moving your blade to the opposite side, edge right, third, made by raising the point, edge right, and so on, including the parry for the head, high five, edge up.

"For every possible attack, there is a parry. You just have to move fast, and against vampires, that means with lightning speed."

"It's sort of like a dance," Cindy said as she went through the moves, now advancing and now retreating.

"It is…It's the dance of death, Cindy," Harold said, "and it only ends when someone's head rolls in the dust, or he falls pierced through the heart."

Harold showed her how to lunge, straightening her sword arm and stepping forward as far as possible, and he had her lunge over and over at a target on the wall to strike the heart painted on it. She moved so fast a human would have seen only a blur but sometimes missed the mark a bit.

"You will need to spend hours of practice to control you movement, so the sword always strikes the heart exactly. Always attack with the point from a distance, with the edge after his parries. Remember the geometry of the sword—the shortest distance between two points is a straight line. Do cuts from the wrist only, unless you have stunned your enemy and need to finish beheading him. Raising your arm makes you vulnerable."

"This is a great work out," Cindy observed, as they were practicing. "Even if I didn't need these skills, the exercise value of it is really great."

That night, Harold and Cindy went clubbing to the Flames of Love and the Bordello, but although they saw many of the immortals, they knew they didn't see any really suspicious behavior. They made a fine pair, the handsome Harold and beautiful Cindy, who wore her miniskirt over black tights. She wore a silver bangle on her wrist, and her pumps were adorned with silver sequins. They danced with various humans and drank from a couple of them, leaving them none the wiser for the experience. At length, they returned home and sent away the babysitter.

Baby sitting and child care for vampire children is a special problem. You can't just call on the teenager next door to do it; instead, you need someone who knows immortal children. They are very strong and tend to be willful. In short, they are a handful. Richard was still very small, but in a couple of years, he would be a real danger to any human, until he could be trained in self-control. Fortunately, Aunt Julia had made someone available to help.

It was that Friday night, at the Bordello Club that Harold and Cindy ran into a pair of immortals from out of town, who split up and danced with various humans. The club was jammed with partying visitors. Waitresses in teddies, baby dolls, and transparent night gowns, showing lots of cleavage and fishnet-clad legs circulated with trays of drinks, while above the dance floor, a mirror ball slowly turned, flashing in the lights. Dancers, most of the women with plunging necklines or transparent tops, dressed in hot pants or minis, jostled each other on the crowded floor. The music of the band almost drowned out conversation.

Harold and Cindy split up to follow them. The man went over to the bar for drinks, for himself and the woman with whom he was dancing and Harold went over to him next to the bar. He was blond, only of medium height, about five feet seven, dressed in a white shirt and charcoal gray flannel slacks. Above the bar were large prints of two famous nude paintings, Goya's *The Naked Maja* and Manet's *Olympia* hung over the long mirror flanked by carved wooden Corinthian columns, making an ornate frame. Below that were countless bottles of every kind of alcoholic beverage (Harold and the stranger and everyone else at the bar were reflected perfectly; it is only a legend that vampires are invisible in mirrors.) There was a crowd at the nineteenth century oak bar, but there happened to be a little space next to the stranger who was waiting for his drinks.

"It's a hot club, isn't it, and the place is really hopping," Harold ventured to the man.

"Yeah, the women here are beautiful," he replied, and then sensing his companion might be immortal, he added "and tasty. Do you come here often?"

"Sure, I live in Las Vegas, and this is one of the best clubs in town. And you are from?"

"Los Angeles, it's close, and this is fun, so I come here for vacations."

At this point, the barkeeper brought him his drinks, set them down on the polished oak, so the stranger paid, and then headed back to the girl.

Harold kept a suspicious eye on him from the distance, and when the vampire left from the back entrance with a girl, he slipped out a side door, so he could observe. Sure enough, the man bit into the neck of his girlfriend, a beautiful brunette clad in a red velvet miniskirt, and Harold prepared to intervene. In a few minutes, however, the guy backed off, licked her neck to close the fang wounds, and returned with her to the club.

Later, Harold met up with Cindy after a fruitless night's observation. Cindy was obviously tired also.

"Yuck," she said. "I felt like a Peeping Tom watching a woman feed on a guy. I don't know how I could have observed it if she had gone into a room to have sex and feed from him at the same time."

"Most rogues don't care about refinements like that," Harold observed. "They enjoy more terrorizing a victim before killing. They feed off fear as much as blood. Let's find dinner ourselves and then head home."

Early next evening, Harold checked in with Delia, to see if she had learned anything more. She was not in her office, and he found her supervising some arrangements for a party in a private room at the club. The staff was setting places at twelve tables covered by airline-themed table cloths. It seemed a new pilot had been hired, and the others in the Las Vegas group were welcoming him with a party.

"Hi," Harold said, "are there any new developments in the case?"

"Yes," Delia said, "come to my office in fifteen minutes, and we'll look at some interesting video."

The video, made the day of the last killings, showed a man, most likely an immortal, who seemed to be about, thirty, of medium stature, dressed in a Hawaiian shirt and jeans with a dark-haired young woman, possibly in her late twenties, exiting toward a parking garage. An hour later, he came back alone, and he stood as though musing, stock still for at least four or five minutes before going into the casino from the hall. His eyes never blinked once. He was surely a vampire. His handsome face had craggy brows, a long straight nose, and a little scruff of beard.

"Maybe that is our killer," Harold remarked. "Have you shown the footage to police?" he asked.

"No, we covered that case up, but of course, we reported it to the Satrap," Delia replied.

"This could be of great help. Thanks a lot for your help, Delia. Make a print from this and show it to your shift leaders. If this guy shows up, have them call me at once on my cellular."

That Friday night, the big break came. Harold and Cindy were once more at the Bordello Club. He dressed and a sports jacket, tie and slacks. She was dressed in a red minidress over black tights. Harold was carrying a silver headed cane, and Cindy, a gold lame purse that matched her slippers, necklace, and bracelet. Harold's cellular rang out three chimes, and he answered the call.

"That guy's back," Delia said. "He and a woman were spotted going into the Flames of Love."

"We'll be there in a flash," Harold said, and he and Cindy took off from the Bordello Club and pulled into the parking garage at the Flames within eight minutes. They headed straight for the security office and the video monitors, where they could check to see which way he left and with whom. He would have to go carefully. He didn't want the immortal to claim he was just doing a normal feeding when security interrupted him.

Harold caught sight of that immortal on a monitor as the vampire approached a girl, maybe eighteen to twenty, maybe a college student and evidently asked her for a dance. The girl was tall and slender, at least six feet, with luxurious black curls falling to her shoulders. After a couple of dances, he went to the bar for drinks and took one back to the girl. *A little alcohol can be a great help in seduction*, Harold mused.

After a few minutes, the vampire slipped out the back door of the club, with the girl he had picked for a feast. Harold quickly left the security room, made his way across the crowded club, and into the alley by a different door.

The alley was dimly lit by a single caged bulb, but you could still hear the band quite well, and the music was loud. There was also the considerable noise of traffic passing on the street. Still, Harold's acute immortal ears could pick up the sound of the conversation between the vampire and his intended victim.

"Let's light up the grass and smoke," she said. "No one can see or hear us back here."

"I'm counting on that, you little cunt," he said. "No one will know it when I rip open your throat and drink your blood to the last drop." His eyes flashed, and his fangs descended. The girl screamed in terror as he seized her and sought her neck with his fangs.

"Stop right there!" Harold shouted. "Let the girl go."

Instantly, the vampire whirled to face Harold, releasing the girl, who stood for a moment, then fled.

"How dare you interrupt me!" he roared. "You, a mere child, dare to thwart me. You will die the true death for your recklessness." With that, he sprang toward Harold with savage power.

Click. Harold pressed down the button on his cane. Harold dropped the cane onto the pavement. With that, Harold raised the point of his sword toward his charging enemy, straightened his arm, and stepped forward extending his arm toward the heart of the leaping vampire.

"Aaagh," said the ancient one as he impaled himself on Harold's point. Then his body hit the pavement with a thud.

Harold looked down as the vampire died the true death. Harold had only a moment to get it in. "I never…ever fight fair."

Cindy was having her own problems. She returned to their car, stripped off the minidress, changed into dark shoes, and picked up her weapons. She had followed the female vampire from the club into the weakly lit parking garage. A spectacular blonde with curves in all the right places and dressed in a wild outfit for clubbing, with a neckline that plunged to the navel and short shorts, she had had no trouble picking up a young, brown-haired college student in jeans and a white shirt. The couple had paid no attention to what seemed a departing patron making her way to her car. The boy was kissing the vampire passionately. Then he came up for air.

"How about coming to my room?" he asked.

"You are so handsome," the lady purred. "You are so handsome, I could just eat you up. In fact, I think I will. Your blood is all mine." Her eyes flashed, and her fangs appeared as she sought out his jugular.

"That's enough!" Cindy shouted from the darkness. "Let him go, now!"

Releasing her victim, the woman turned. "Who do you think you are disturbing me at my dinner? I'm going to kill you instead, just for messing with me." With that, she focused on Cindy and charged toward her.

Thunk went the arrow from the bow, and it tore an x-shaped hole through the woman, missing her heart by millimeters. The woman stopped and looked down in amazement at her wound.

Then, as she began to heal, she looked up and charged straight towards her enemy.

The second arrow found its mark exactly, and the immortal died the true death, collapsing into a pile only two feet from Cindy.

"Wow," Cindy said. "Thank God that's over."

Delia sent a cleanup squad outfitted as an emergency medical team to quietly remove the bodies. With that, the rogue attacks ceased and the vampire and human communities breathed a collective sigh of relief.

One day while at work in his office, Harold heard a knock at his door. He opened it and was surprised to see Ronald Andrews, the Satrap of Nevada himself.

"I came to thank you for your service to our community," the Satrap said, "and I want to consult with you about another matter as well," he said.

"Just let me know what you need," Harold said, "and how I may be of help."

"I have a great project in mind, and when I succeed, I would like to name you as the new Satrap of Nevada."

"Only the King, He Whose Name No Mortal May Speak, could do that," Harold observed.

"That's right," the Satrap replied. "I mean to replace the King myself."

"Under our laws you have the right to challenge him to combat," Harold said, "but I would prefer to steer clear of politics. Think it over. He is a mighty immortal, but I will say nothing to anyone."

"Look," Ronald said. "I'm going to need your assistance to do this. Whoever is not for me is against me."

"I respect your rights under the law," Harold replied, "but I will not be a part of any plan to ambush our ruler. I don't want to even hear it. And if I do I cannot promise to keep silent about that."

"That's the way it is then?" Ronald asked.

"That just the way it is," Harold answered.

II. Blood Spatters
Shatter the Peace

The Satrap's council was held in one of the most elegant old houses in Las Vegas, Rancho Circle, a district where big name show performers, politicians, and others of the city's elite lived. It was a huge single-story ranch house evidently constructed in the 1950s, still elegant in its old age. Brick veneer construction and large windows, with faux shutters gave it a look of distinction, and it had a shake roof. Lights shown from every window that night as the conspirators met. Four months had passed since Harold had defeated the rogues, and since then, no word had passed between overlord and vassal.

They sat around a long table, and before each sat a glass of warm, freshly drawn human blood. On the table, there was a centerpiece of night blooming cactus flowers. Ronald Andrews, Satrap of Nevada, sat at its head flanked by Jerry Richardson and Harry Reeves. Representatives from almost every night club and vampire enterprise in Nevada sat along its sides, but a few were conspicuous by their absence, Delia and Julia, and Harold in particular. There were chairs along the sides of the room for less important supporters, in the center an elegant Persian carpet lay over the hardwood floor, under the table legs, and hanging above the table in the room's center, a crystal chandelier ablaze with light.

"You have all been receptive to my plan to give Nevada a larger role in vampire affairs, to cut its taxes, and provide important new privileges, that would mean more money for us all. The present King is unworthy of us, and I will replace him and provide a more favorable regime, but we must eliminate those who are apt to support him. I asked for a list of all enemies who should die from each of you. Now we will collect the lists and remove the names of those not really firm supporters of the present regime."

Every representative handed in a list of names written on a sheet of paper, and they all passed them to the head of the table where the Satrap scanned the names of the persons each had proposed to proscribe. Ronald examined each of the dozen lists.

"Let's consider these names one by one."

"Delia, why would we sentence this vampire to destruction?" the Satrap asked maybe mostly for the sake of form. "She had never interfered with my government and in fact has helped me more than once."

Norman Winters of Reno's Club Blood stood to speak.

"The King is of her line, so she would resent anyone killing him, bide her time, and then send another one of hers to challenge any new ruler. Or maybe she would become a center for plots against the crown. No monarch could trust her, at least unless he were of her lineage. Delia should die."

"Winters said Delia should die. How say the rest of you. Hands up those of you who would strike her down."

The room was suddenly dead silent. A dozen hands rose.

"Then she shall die by your decision," said the Satrap. He read off another name.

"Harold Halbmann, why should this immortal die? He has supported our rule in Nevada well, and he defeated a plot to assassinate a US president, a plot that would have been a disaster for our businesses here in the Silver State."

Richardson rose to address the conspirators. "Harold is also of Delia's line, and when offered a chance to join us, he refused. He said he doesn't want to get involved with vampire politics. We just can't trust a man like that. Sooner or later, he will go to the King with information about our plans. He must die."

Genevieve, the satrap's wife, a pretty former waitress he had turned, a blue-eyed woman with shoulder length black hair, only five feet six inches tall, rose to say her piece. "I remember an immortal with a new son. Maybe he doesn't want to risk the child's life, if the King were to retaliate, should our challenge fail. I understand he recognized that the Satrap has a legal right to challenge the King. If he will stay out of it, why kill such a useful member of our community?"

Richardson replied, "We just can't believe an immortal like that. If he exposes us and the King kills us he will surely become the next satrap. Kill him now before he gets any more information or ideas of what we may do."

"How many favor death for Halbmann?" asked the Satrap. "Let's see your hands if you do."

Ten conspirators raised their hands.

"It's decided then. Halbmann must die too," decided the Satrap who looked at the next name.

"Why should Julia Strange die?" Ronald asked. "She is the soul of gentleness, a vampiress sparing even to humans, our natural food—a woman who would never kill anyone of humankind or of ours?"

Winters said, "She is also of Delia's line, and although she would never kill anyone, I agree. She might get wind of our plot. After all, what better way to learn what is about to happen than run a whorehouse? Even the Nazis understood that. Men talk when they visit women and women—women just talk. Kill her too, I say."

And so the conspirators continued on to decide on a list of all those proscribed, marked for death to clear the way for the new regime. In the end they had a list of fifteen names, many of them on the staff of the Bordello Club or Flames of Love.

"No one must suspect that these killings are part of a vampire conspiracy, so I think we should hire human killers to take them out," the Satrap said. "We will inform them exactly what to do to be sure that all those marked for death truly die. When they have finished our work we will turn them or kill those we hired according to their deserts."

A week later Harold was on his way home suddenly a car pulled out of a side street, where it had been hidden behind abandoned houses, and right in front of him, stopping to completely block his way. That activated his car's collision avoidance system and caused it to brake to a stop. Seconds later, another car crossed into the road behind him, blocking any retreat.

A machine-pistol burst shattered his windshield and bullets whistled around his head. Harold dropped to the floor of his vehicle, grabbed a pistol, opened the door, and rolled out onto the ground. He looked out toward the shooters from beneath the car. They had fired from the windows of an abandoned house. Quickly, Harold took out his cellular and dialed 911. Then he grasped his weapon and waited.

Three unkempt men in long hair, scraggly beards, and fatigues emerged from the house, two holding their guns at the ready and the third grasping a machete. As Harold waited, he caught some of their conversation. "I got him good and fair, and I deserve the bonus," one of the gunmen said. "He's a vampire, you idiot. He won't really be dead until I cut off his head," said the man carrying the machete.

When they were quite close, Harold shot down the nearest gunman and shifted his aim to the second. The second gunman shot then, and a bullet passed through Harold's left shoulder at the very moment he fired and took down his enemy. The third man turned to flee, but Harold aimed at his knee and shattered it with a bullet causing him to fall. Harold's wound was already starting to heal.

He saw one of the gunmen struggle to rise after a few minutes, and then, Harold heard the sound of police cars approaching the scene, their sirens screaming. He realized he was going to have to do a lot of explaining to the Las Vegas Sheriff's Department, that it might even charge him for possessing and using a weapon.

Well, he thought, *it's better to be tried by twelve rather than be carried by six.*

There could be no greater contrast than between Detectives Brian O'Connell and Angel de la Cruz. They were both in their 30s, but all similarity ended there. The first was a beefy 230-

pound blond, red-nosed Irishman, who had been a patrol officer in New York State, and had come west in search of a detective's shield, the other was dark-skinned, black haired, wiry 165-pound California born Hispanic. The room was totally bare. There were no windows, only a table, three straight back chairs and a single florescent light in the ceiling.

"What kind of business were you involved in with the gunmen?" O'Brian asked. "Did you short them in a payment for drugs?" His face seemed more livid.

Then Angel chimed in, "People don't mount attacks like this for nothing. You must have done something to make them mad. What was it?" he said with a sneer.

"Look," Harold said, "I don't know these men. I never saw them before, and I am not involved in any kind of criminal activity that would explain their attack."

Over and over again, Harold explained to them that he did not know the men who attacked him and that he was not in an illegal business of any kind. After three hours, they finally released him but kept his weapon for evidence. They told him that considering the circumstances, he would probably not be charged for carrying a loaded weapon concealed in his vehicle. "Just don't leave town," Sergeant Joe Larkin said, "and if you remember anything, call me at once."

He was just leaving when the call came in. Someone had attacked people partying at the Flames of Love night club killing seven patrons and three members of the staff. The killer had fled out the door as soon as he finished firing. The police SWAT team was running out of the station for its vehicles. And the metropolitan police had issued an all-points bulletin, seeking to arrest the shooter before he could leave the area.

Actually, Harold mused, it would probably be better if he did leave town, the police prohibition notwithstanding. More importantly, he decided that Cindy and Richard should leave town at once and head for a safe place. The problem with the

Satrap was serious; any direct act of rebellion was suicide. The Satrap would naturally know nothing about today's events, but it seemed crystal clear to Harold that he was behind them. His assassins would try again for sure, and his family would certainly be in danger. He would have to warn others too. He hoped Delia had survived the attack. Yet he could not prove the Satrap was plotting against his King, and any charge could easily be turned against him. Immortal protocol required obedience to his overlord. Now if he could prove a plot against the King, that would be different.

"What happened?" Cindy asked when Harold came through the door. "I was expecting you home hours ago."

"I was attacked on the way home, fired on with a machine pistol. I waited for them to check out their shot and hit two with my return fire. The SOBs even hit me once, but one is dead, and the others are in police custody now."

"So the Satrap had decided to murder us," Cindy observed. "The worst thing about being an immortal is that vampire politics really suck, something you told me before."

"You and Richard need to clear out of here fast," Harold said. "Go to some place you know from your youth, but stay clear of your relatives. You're supposed to be dead, after all. I am really, really, sorry that our son will have to dodge the Satrap the same way I had to hide from the King when I was growing up."

"I will stand and fight beside you, and we will protect our son. There is no need to hide him," Cindy said. "I love you both and will defend you to the last."

"I know you will, and I love you," said Harold, "but we can't risk our son. He is still so vulnerable and the Satrap will be utterly ruthless. You both must go."

After much more discussion, they decided that Cindy and their son should go to a cabin that Harold had obtained under another name in the north. She would slip away in their car with its heavily tinted windows in daytime, as though she were going shopping or something.

That way, the danger from immortals would be less.

That last evening, before their separation, Harold held Cindy firmly in his arms, and he kissed her tenderly first, then with increasing passion. They both knew that it might be along while until they could safely see each other again, so they surged together with the same energy that mortal couples sometimes know on the eve of a soldier's departure for a war. Hope and fear struggled in their hearts, and they were filled with a desire to make every moment together memorable and fearful that this brief time might be their last together. At length, the flames of love subsided into tender caresses touched with sadness. Then too soon it was time for Cindy's good-bye.

That evening, after Cindy and Richard had left, Harold visited the Flames of Love and found that Delia had escaped the attack although two members of the club's immortal staff had been shot and then decapitated with a machete, something that was puzzling police investigators.

A visit to the House of Strange brought Harold to Julia, hitherto untouched by the Satrap's assassins.

"Why have you come?" she asked.

"I suggest you disappear," he said. "I fear my enemies will try to kill you," he said.

"Why on earth would they do that?' Julia asked. "I never bother anyone."

"Yes, but because you belong to Delia's line and are within the Satrap's easy reach you are in danger. If there is someone who can conduct business for you for a while, I suggest you get out of town for a vacation until this whole business blows over," Harold remarked.

Then, he filled her in on the events of the last few days, and it all became much clearer. The Satrap was out of control, and sooner or later, the King would kill him, but until then, there would be great danger. Julia would leave town, but Harold realized how much he and his wife had leaned on her for help with different things. Certainly, her stand in could help too, but it just wouldn't be the same.

Meanwhile, Harold decided to move into town, where any attack would be more obvious, and he would be closer to his work. Whenever his enemies struck, he asked his friends to let him know. In his country residence, he would just lock up until he and his family could safely return. Meanwhile, he could move around and use resting places in the several buildings he owned in town, complicating the task or the Satrap's assassins, vampire or human. He reflected again on his wonderful wife; he knew she would fight beside him, die to save him or her son, and that few vampires or mortals would ever know such love.

When they struck the Bordello Club, a friend, Bobby Jones, called Harold on his cellular.

"Come quick, Harold. They are shooting up the Bordello Club. One of the shooters asked for Delia, and then they opened fire."

Harold arrived just as the shooters were fleeing the club. He shot out the tire on their SUV, which they abandoned in the parking garage. The last of the assassins to scramble out fell to Harold's arrow; three others reached the street and exchanged fire with police as they arrived on the scene. Harold stashed his weapons in his trunk, then shrank back into a corner of the parking garage and stood stock still until the police finished their search. Then he left, disappearing into the darkness.

"It's been a violent evening," the newscaster said, looking soberly from the TV screen. "First at least, three attackers opened fire in the Bordello Club, a nightclub on the Las Vegas strip, leaving two dead and seven wounded, then they fled. Somehow, their rear tire blew out before they left the garage, and someone killed one of them with an arrow. The others reached the street and two exchanged fire with the police and were killed. One of them is still at large. So far, none has been identified. Minutes later, in nearby Nye County, a man attacked girls and visitors to a brothel and killed four persons before a guard shot him down. Notes identified the group responsible as Nevadans Against Glorification of Vice." Harold turned off the set and went to his chosen resting place.

"Never send mortals to do a vampire's work," Ronald exclaimed, and he turned around in his office chair to look at his confidant. "Jerry, those guys you hired to kill Delia, Harold, and Julia make the Keystone cops look like experts. So far, you have only eliminated three of the fifteen, and those are the least important. Fortunately, those in police custody know nothing. I want the rest of that scum dead, and I mean really dead—not turned. They don't deserve what we promised to pay them, not one."

"You have already attracted too much attention to things here in Vegas," Genevieve said.

She was attractively, dressed in a blue tank dress with a scoop neck, pantyhose, and heels. "We don't want to draw the King's attention to this city or state. He might become suspicious."

"I agree," the Satrap noted. Then he turned to Jerry Richardson again. "You are going to have to hunt Harold and the others down and really kill them one by one Take your time but find and kill all of them. Harold has a company to run; that should give you a better chance to find him. No one knows where Delia and Julia have gone, and Harold's family disappeared too. Delia and Julia have turned over their work to others and could hide for centuries.

"I want our people watching every one of his places of business, and I want someone in every vampire-run enterprise in Las Vegas. I want to know when Harold or any of the others is spotted. This time, our strike must go unnoticed, and our enemies just disappear."

Harold left the office of Halbmann Motors next day and headed toward that of Halbmann Enterprises where he would meet Jack Springer, his deputy, who would have to carry a heavier load now that his boss had to dodge the mortal killers dispatched by the Satrap. Harold noted that the same car kept turning up behind him. He was being shadowed, he decided.

When it came time to go to ground, it was a blazing hot Las Vegas day, at least 110 degrees outside, and Harold pondered his choices. He could nap in the attic, which would be way too hot, or in the back of his air-conditioned office or in the cellar, both of which were fine for his rest. The secretary, Camille Jones and Jack Springer, could handle any business while he slept. Just to be on the safe side, he decided, considering the tail, he'd tell them he was napping in the back room as usual, then descend to the place he had set up in the cellar, against the far wall behind boxes of brochures for his different businesses.

The cot was far from that comfortable, but then, being immortal has its advantages, and Harold took off his shoes, pulled a sheet over his body, and was soon dead to the world. About three in the afternoon, his alarm went off vibrating silently against his side and recalling him to life.

The scream shocked Harold into motion, he grabbed his Glock, shot up the stairs and saw the locked door to his back room had been broken down. From the darkened room he could see three powerful men. One dressed in a logoed T-shirt and jeans, held Jack with his arms behind his back and two others were giving their attention to Camille.

One held her arms behind her back while the other had removed her top, pulled off her bra, and was holding a glowing cigarette in one hand and deciding where to apply it on her breast.

"No more lies, just tell me the truth where is Harold Halbmann? Tell me right now or I will hurt you again," he snarled. Harold overheard his thoughts: *As soon as I get rid of Harold we're all going to have a little fun, fuck this women and kill both of them.*

"Right here," responded Harold sweetly, holding his weapon on the cigarette bearer, and then, he shouted, "Let them go now!"

When they saw the pistol, they let Jack and Camille go. One man blanched white with fear. The other reached for a handgun.

The shot was deafening, but the man staggered back against the wall then slid down to the floor.

Harold looked at the two would be murderers, one trembling with fear, the other stunned. Looking at the shaking fellow, he spoke. "You," he said, "get out of here. Go tell your bosses you failed."

Instantly, the man dropped his machete fled out the door.

"You," Harold said, looking at the man who had been torturing Camille, who stood unshaven, square jawed, and long haired, but only of average height, clad in a lumberjack shirt and cargo pants. "You will be my guest for dinner. Usually, I prefer dinner companions of a more pleasant aspect, but for you, I will make an exception this one time."

When the man saw Harold's eyes glitter and his fangs descend, he was terrified. They hadn't told him what a terrible creature he was hunting.

"Stay, right here," he told the man as he looked into his eyes.

Then he talked to Camille and Jack, mesmerizing both, and he told them to go home for the rest of the day and that nothing had really happened. After that, he picked up the phone and called the number at the Flames of Love, then gave an extension number.

"Yes?" said the voice on the other end of the line.

"Clean up on aisle six," Harold said.

"Wet or dry?" the voice asked.

"One wet, one dry," Harold said.

"How many total?"

"Two," Harold responded.

Harold knew that the cleaning crew would come that night and remove the two corpses, one dead from a gunshot, one drained dry, and wipe down the site of their deaths. When the sun rose tomorrow there would be no evidence of the violent struggle that cost two men their lives, nor would the Department of Homeland Security be any the wiser because of his call.

Harold knew that they would surely be a follow up to the attack, so when slipped away from Halbmann Enterprises that night after the cleaners left, he took his saber and a crossbow from concealment in a locked box in his vehicle and placed them where he could get them in a hurry. This time, he found refuge in a warehouse he owned, about three blocks from the Stratosphere Tower. Finding him in there would involve an extensive search where a security system had already been installed to guard against theft.

What a mess, Harold realized. There must be spies watching every vampire business in town, and they were obviously trying to shadow him also. They would come again, and despite the difficulties, they would try to get him here, he decided. He would plan on it.

The Satrap and his inner circle were meeting once more in his office. They were seated in a semicircle of chairs before his desk. Word had just come that the latest attempt on Harold had failed once more.

"What do we do now?" the Satrap said. "Attacking Harold in the warehouse could be tricky since it is well-alarmed. There are many places inside he could be. Any suggestions?"

"Could we suggest peace to him on condition that he stay neutral," Genevieve suggested.

"I think he would accept a treaty for the sake of his wife and child."

"It's too late for that," the Satrap observed. "The only way now is to kill him at that warehouse where he is hiding."

"If we cut off the power, we would shut down the alarm system, and the darkness is not a problem for immortals," Jerry suggested.

"I've a better idea," Harry offered. "Let's burn the whole building down. We would risk nothing and could jump him when he fled from the flames."

"What about the danger of being recorded on the security cameras of neighboring buildings?" Norman asked.

"Couldn't we cut power to the whole neighborhood?" suggested Harry.

"We could, but that would draw attention too soon," remarked the Satrap. "We would have to do it only moments before going into Harold's warehouse. Also, does anyone know if the building has a generator to deal with power outages?"

"I don't think so," Jerry said. "Let's just cut the power and go for it. If we see any obvious security cameras on outside buildings, we'll blast them with gunfire."

That night, Harold noticed when the power to his building went off because an alarm sounded, informing him that the attack had started. Seconds later, Richardson's men forced the side door to the warehouse. Five immortals accompanied him. Two others forced the main door.

As Harold planned, three minutes later, a steel portcullis dropped in place behind each group with a soft crump. Normally, they would have been lowered when the building closed as extra security. Harold had kept them raised.

Security at the warehouse had always meant sixty-seven-year old, balding, retired metro policeman Elmer David, of average height and build with a pot belly to match his years. He wore a uniform and carried an ancient Colt official police.38 special revolver. Harold would always remember his instructions to Elmer that evening.

"Take a folding chair and go out and sit in the alley behind the warehouse; it should be a comfortable 80 degrees. Peak around the side of the building once and a while and if you see a door ajar or broken, call 911 and report a burglary in progress. Once you do that, go home, do not, I repeat, do not under any circumstances try to stop the burglars. Just go home."

Harold, once the assassins were in his warehouse, stole out the window onto the fire escape, and he closed the folding security bars and snapped shut the padlock behind him. Now he had them where he wanted them, locked into a warehouse where they had no right to be, and police were on their way. He had taken out a considerable part of the hostile immortals, and the King would not be happy that they were exposed as would be killers.

Meanwhile, the night guard had called in his report and was leaving the scene when he encountered a huge immortal whom I will call Goliath. Goliath, mostly a shadow, but sometimes seen in the moonlight or a street light, held a Japanese katana before him with both hands. He had been left to guard Jerry's SUV, in a neighborhood that wasn't the best, and with his superior vampire vision he spotted a figure scurrying away in the darkness and advanced to challenge the man. Elmer saw a giant with a sword advance on him.

"Stop or I'll shoot," he warned after drawing his revolver.

"Stupid mortal!" Goliath roared.

Elmer held his revolver with both hands and aimed at the center of the dark mass charging toward him. He fired five times. *Bam! Bam! Bam! Bam! Bam!* Four of the five bullets actually hit Goliath, and the sting of those bullets made the vampire angry—really, really, angry.

Up swung the great sword, up and down. The blade cut right through Elmer's shoulder blade into his lungs and heart. Elmer collapsed onto the pavement. At that moment, his wife became a widow, his two children, fatherless. For once, David with a slingshot had not defeated Goliath with his sword.

Harold heard his guard's revolver bark five times as Elmer engaged the intruder, and then, there was silence. Harold drew his sword, and descended with it in his right hand, point over his left shoulder, edge to the front. When he reached the lower steps of the fire escape, they slid down to the street and then rose again as Harold stepped off and ran toward the sound.

When Harold saw Goliath, he straightened his arm, turned his hand palm to the right and the saber edge up. Then he ran forward with his point toward the giant. Goliath swung his sword back to the right for a stupendous cut.

Harold was quite close when he saw the blade start forward and dropped into a long lunge, and his left hand touched the ground, and he thrust his blade up toward the giant's heart; he felt the air as the blade that would have severed his head passed inches above it. Then his point pierced Goliath's chest missing his heart by millimeters. Goliath's face caught in the light of the street lamps, blanched, and his jaw dropped. Four bullet wounds and a nearly fatal thrust near the heart was a lot even for a vampire to repair, and he was stunned for a moment.

Quickly, Harold recovered and hacked at his enemy's neck once and then again, and finally, his great head rolled into the street. For Goliath, it was over.

Jerry Richardson, meanwhile, was having his own problems. He couldn't find Harold anywhere. Then he and his confederates heard police sirens in the distance.

"Burn him out then," Harry suggested. "That way, you will kill him wherever he is hiding."

"Do it," Jerry said.

Harry threw the Molotov cocktail against a stack of boxes, and the flames covered them.

"Let's get out of here," Jerry said.

When they got to the exit, they found it barred, and they could not raise the gate.

"There must be a switch to raise the door," Jerry said. "Let's find it."

Precious minutes went by until they found the switch. Jerry flipped it but nothing happened. The flames were spreading everywhere.

"That's right," Norman said. "We cut the power."

"There is an auxiliary generator over here!" Harry noticed.

Jerry tried to start it, but it wouldn't turn on.

"No wonder," said Norman. "There is no gas in the tank."

"Look for a fire escape. There has to be one!" Jerry exclaimed with desperation. "We have to get out of here."

The police wanted to charge Harold with deliberately luring his enemies into the building and then burning it, but they couldn't prove he was there, and the fire investigators reported that the blaze was set close to where the intruders were; they had set fire to the structure themselves and then burned alive. There was also a dead security guard and a headless corpse. Surely, there was some kind of a fight, but Harold claimed he knew nothing about it.

The Satrap's phone rang the two days later; it was an encrypted call from the King. He picked up the phone.

"Why," asked He Whose Name No Mortal May Speak. "Why are you trying to kill Harold Halbmann, Protector of the South?"

"He's a traitor against us and must die."

"It appears you need help. Really you must be more careful of exposing us. I am sending some of my men to help you."

"Thank you, Sire," he replied, groaning inwardly. The last thing he needed now was a royal inquiry into the circumstances of Harold's treason.

Later, the Satrap met with his advisors, at least what was left of them. Genevieve, his wife, was also with him.

"Harold is a real pain in my backside. How can I neutralize him?"

"There is one thing you have forgotten. That is that Harold is married and has a son," Genevieve said. "Get control of them, and he will do anything you ask. Not that you ever take my advice, but I would say find the woman and her son, seize them, and you will have him over a barrel."

"I think you might be right," Ronald Andrews admitted. "That's exactly what we must do."

III. CHERCHEZ LA FEMME

Three days after the last police interrogation Harold was back in his office at Halbmann Motors when Delia appeared with a very serious face.

"I must warn you," said the blond beauty, "that the Satrap has accused you of treason against him and the King, and He Whose Name No Mortal May Speak is sending reinforcements to back up his deputy here in Nevada."

"Who just happens to be planning to kill him and take over the monarchy himself," noted Harold.

"Quite so," Delia replied. "We just can't prove he's the conspirator right now."

"What a shame, all those minions of his perished in the fire. I was hoping to get something out of them."

"It was a brilliant plan, Harold. You are really a great vampire warrior as I knew you'd be, not at all like your bookish uncle. Too bad those fools set your warehouse on fire."

"I hadn't counted on them doing anything that stupid."

"Remember although no one must know where I've gone to ground," Delia said. "If you need our help just contact the staff at one of our clubs, and I'll send whatever help I can. Bye."

With that, she turned and vanished into the street in a few moments blending with the passersby.

That evening, Harold's cellular chimed three times, and he took it up.

"Yes?" he answered.

"Darling," Cindy asked, "are you okay? How did you get out of your warehouse alive? Are you still hiding from him?" The questions came in a torrent.

"One thing at a time, my love." Harold said. "I'm fine. I slipped out after I had trapped them. I never imagined they would set the building on fire." One by one, he answered each of her questions.

"Also, I owe a lot to Elmer David," Harold noted. "He put four bullets into one of them before he died, and that slowed him down just enough that I could kill the vampire. We have to do something to help his widow and children."

"How is Richard doing?"

"He is growing every day," she said, "and he really misses his papa."

"I love you," he said, "and above all, I want you to stay safe. Don't call on your cellular. Remember they can use GPS technology to locate a call, and that wouldn't be safe for you."

"Yeah, I know," she answered. I love you so much. I just cannot wait for this to be over. Good-bye for now."

Four weeks later, the Satrap was talking to his advisors in his office. He had promoted two vampires, Harry Donaldson and Ernesto Mendez, to replace his lost body guards and advisors, and he had turned seven men into immortals to fill the gaps left by the losses in the fire. Included among their number were technicians who were helping him trace the phone calls Cindy was making to Harold. Richard Towers explained the situation to his sire.

"Cindy seems to be hiding out somewhere around Cedar City Utah. There are a lot of cabins up there a person could buy or rent. Most of Cindy's calls are coming from a twenty-mile radius around the city. She could be hiding in town, but I don't think so."

The Satrap considered this and then made a decision. He looked at the circle of faces around him, most of them, with the exception of Genevieve, were new.

"I am going to reduce our surveillance of the nightclubs around town here and sent those people up to Cedar City and have them patrol the gas stations around there. I'll encourage the people the King sent to watch the local clubs. We'll make copies of one of photos from Richard's first birthday bash and give one to each hunter. There is a reason vampires don't like to be photographed. She is new, however, and didn't know any better. Whoever sees her must hang back a little and follow her to determine her hiding place. I want to send a four-man team up there on standby to be ready whenever we find her."

Ernesto reported three weeks later that a clerk at One Stop for Everything remembered seeing Cindy there not two weeks before.

He remembered her especially because of the rambunctious kid who seemed to want to get into everything.

"She really had her hands full. The kid had just started to walk, but talk about mobility, he wanted to go everywhere and grab everything," reported the clerk.

"Call us at once if she comes in again," Ernesto said. "Her ex-husband wants his kid back. He has shared custody rights, but she just took the boy and disappeared. Call me at 702-645-5529. There's $50 cash in it for you if you do."

Once they figured out the pattern of her calls, Harry realized they'd be able to grab her and threaten to stake her and the boy out in the desert in exchange for Harold turning himself in to the Satrap, to be executed on a charge of treason against his Monarch.

Meanwhile, back in Las Vegas, Edward Zumbaski, one of the Satrap's operatives was explaining the search for Harold to Emile Claron, an agent of the King.

"Harold often frequents our nightclubs here in Vegas as he has connections with Delia and others in that world. In fact, we are also looking for Delia in connection with his conspiracy and Julia as well, you know, the madam at the House of Strange."

"Delia is involved in plans to harm the king?" Emile asked. "That seems a little odd. I thought she was the soul of loyalty to Him Whose Name No Mortal May Speak."

"When there is a crown to win, and so much power at stake, even ancient loyalties are often sacrificed," Edward observed. "So if you see anyone on this list of the proscribed, arrest him or her, or at least, let us know where the person can be found so we can move in. Treason must be stamped out."

Emile looked at the list of fifteen names, four struck off. Then he put it into his pocket and walked out. He was going to visit half a dozen clubs tonight in his quest to arrest the fugitives.

Harold answered his phone a week later on the second ring. It was so good to hear from his love and to listen to the sound of her voice once more.

"Harold, there is something wrong here," she said. "The clerk at this little store where I sometimes buy groceries said that a man is looking for me and even showed him my picture. He said he was working for my ex-husband who claimed I had abducted his son. He offered the clerk money for information about me and told him to call if he saw me again. I explained to him it wasn't true, and that if I had done that the police would be hunting for me not some private investigator. I said the man was a violent abuser who used to beat me up constantly until I left him."

"Go home right now, Cindy, and stay there until I come for you. Keep your weapons handy. You and Richard lay low," Harold responded, frightened for his wife and son. He ran for his vehicle and started its engine. He would drive fast, right to the legal limit, and even faster once he was out of town.

Archeologos II, He Whose Name No Mortal May Speak, was troubled. He could understand how an ambitious rising, vampire warrior like Harold could plot to seize his throne, even though victory in a fair contest would bring much more prestige. Delia was ancient and devious, but it was weird that the mother of his line would seek to destroy one of her own progeny. He found Julia's treason absolutely inexplicable. Why would a vampire who nearly had to be destroyed because she refused to kill, plot against the throne? Julia had accepted work where, though she had to bleed men, she never had to kill them. Taken together, they seemed three very unlikely principal conspirators. There was something rotten in Las Vegas, the King decided, something that called for a royal investigation. The King placed a call to Emile Claron in Las Vegas.

"Emile," the monarch said, "thank you for your report about the treason case in Nevada. we want you to continue with your search for those on the Satrap's list, but we also want you and the boys to snoop around and find out what's really going on over there. This case stinks. Under no conditions allow the execution of anyone for treason until we decide all the facts are clear."

Still the King knew that if the Satrap's men captured the suspects first, it would be impossible to insure they were not killed right away anyway. Even his direct order would not shield them from death for "resisting arrest" or some alleged accident. Still he picked up the phone for his secure line and called his Satrap in Nevada.

At dusk, the hit team converged on the little cabin in the pine grove. There were four vampires armed with swords, quite enough Harry thought, to take out a mere newbie vampire.

One of them had seen her at the store, which they had watched even though the manager had not called them; no reward for him then, except maybe death once the operation was complete.

The cabin was really nice in a rustic way, it had three rooms, solar panels on the roof, and a wind turbine for electricity. It had a well and nearby a small mountain stream splashed over the rocks adding its music to the night sounds.

The first team member crashed through the door, and suddenly a brilliant, blinding light flashed and an arrow made a direct hit on his heart. Harry and the second member of his team went through the door and pushed over the spotlight on its tripod. The vampire was really angry that Cindy had taken out his comrade and with his free right hand he swung his katana at Cindy who caught the blade, raising her saber over her head, edge up in a parry of high five, and followed with a slash at his side under his right sword arm. He screamed when the stinging cut connected but seized the hilt of his sword with his now free left hand under the right and raised his blade with both hands for a mighty cut. Cindy hurled herself against the back wall and beyond his reach, kicked a straight back chair that had fallen over towards her assailant's feet to complicate his advance, and brought her saber back into guard.

Harry had gone around the fight into the bedroom where he grabbed little Richard, brought the boy back out, and held a knife at his throat. He screamed, "Stop now or I'll take the head off your brat."

Cindy dropped her saber and glared at her enemies. She had hoped that Harold would be here more than ever, but she had finished her call less than a half hour ago.

They grabbed her and chained her with silver, then put her and Richard into their SUV and started off. Little Richard kicked and hit at them ferociously. He didn't like to be held tightly and confined, and his strength far exceeded that of any normal two-year-old human. If they had been human, it would have hurt, but the vampires only laughed at him.

"Feisty little bastard, isn't he?" Harry said.

At that moment, Richard kicked so hard that when his foot struck the door, it smashed through the lining and left a dent that could be seen from the outside. After that, the vampires were less amused by the infant's antics.

When Harold arrived, he found the cabin door open, the chair on its side and the fallen tripod. Cindy's crossbow was on the floor and her sword as well. Most Cindy's clothing was still in the open suitcase, where she had been packing it and a few items remained in the bureau, some smaller things. A comb and hairbrush were scattered about in the bedroom, and Richard's crib was overturned. Obviously, his enemies had his wife and his son.

Harold got into his SUV and thought about the situation. They will not hold her around here so far from the Satrap's domain. They are on their way back to Las Vegas, and there is only one really convenient route there from St. George—Interstate 15. It passes through the Virgin River Gorge, where the road winds on a narrow shelf high above the Virgin River. That might be the ideal place to stop them. Of course, they could go north and circle around, but that would be too long, or they could have driven east, and then around by the south, which would have been equally out of the way.

Harold headed south on I-15, increasing his speed to 95 miles an hour and even 115 at times he had to get ahead of them. If he could identify the vehicle, he might be able to block it and maybe challenge the men to battle. They wanted him dead, and they now had his full attention. He was hoping that the party that seized his wife was small, and maybe one or more might have been killed in the fighting that obviously took place. He was going over 100 when he heard the patrol car put on its siren. He had been so intent on catching up to the kidnappers that he had entirely forgotten that the roads were patrolled by police.

Harold slowed and pulled over. The last thing he needed was another confrontation with police. Fortunately, the policeman was a lone highway patrolman. Harold thought, *That's just like the police, exactly where you need them*. Now he had no chance of catching up to the kidnappers.

"You're driving like a maniac," the policeman said. "Step out of the car. Are you drunk?" "Not at all," Harold said.

The policeman insisted on doing a field sobriety test, which of course showed the vampire was completely sober. The officer still wasn't satisfied. He radioed in to check just in case some criminal was making his escape from a bank robbery. Finally, he came back without finding a clue as to whom he was talking with.

"You were really driving way too fast," he said, making eye contact with Harold. "I am going to have to write you up for this."

"I did nothing wrong," Harold replied, looking intently at the officer and bending his will. "It was an emergency."

After a moment, the policemen said, "Really, you did nothing wrong. It was an emergency." Then he tore up the ticket he had been writing.

"You may go. Now drive safely," he said as Harold pulled back onto the highway. Harold knew it was too late to catch the men who had his wife and son, and he drove back to Las Vegas with a heavy heart.

Harold slipped into the office of Halbmann Motors and turned on his answering machine, but there was still no message. How could he save his family? They probably wouldn't hurt Cindy or Richard, while he was free, at least not at first. Later on—later on, who knows. Harold wondered, how could he prove the Satrap's treason? How could he prove his own innocence and how could he establish the Satrap's guilt. What must follow would be savage and cruel, he knew, with vampires staked out naked in the sun to slowly burn in agony. He wouldn't have wished that for anybody, but the Satrap had simplified the issue—your family or mine. If he were executed for his so-called plot against the Satrap, Cindy would be implicated too and would have to suffer the same horrible fate. And as for Richard, kings were not accustomed to treat the children of traitors kindly. *Vampire society could be savage, and we call ourselves immortals*, he thought, seeing the irony in it.

After stewing in his own juice for a while, he returned to one of his offices and picked up the phone again. This time, there was a message on it.

"We have your wife and son. Turn yourself in to us for trial and execution. The King guarantees you will not be executed until we have completed a fair hearing," the message on his answering machine said. "If you do that your wife and son will be released after your execution. Otherwise, we cannot answer for their safety."

What rubbish! Harold thought. *If I turn myself in to them, I'll be killed during my capture. My wife will be executed as my coconspirator along with Delia and poor Julia. All of them are completely innocent, of course. And it's all because I wouldn't go along with the murder of the King. I wish so much that they would have just left me alone. They just had to drag me into their dirty little scheme. Even had they succeeded, their monarchy would have begun under a cloud, a king who was not mighty enough to prevail in single combat but was only in office because of trickery. He wouldn't have lasted even a century before a more powerful vampire challenged him.*

There is only way to get out of this alive is to get my hands on some of the conspirators and literally wring the truth from them—get them to say some incriminating things that will prove the Satrap is responsible for this mess.

How am I going to do that? How can I save my family? Where can I find the resources for my plans? And, meanwhile how am I going to avoid the agents of the Satrap and the King until I can do those things?

There was only one way to prevail, and Harold knew it. Delia could help. He would need immortals from the club and maybe even Julia could assist him.

We all have to work together...I simply cannot save us alone.

IV. THE TRUTH WINS OUT

Harold managed to send word to Delia through her nightclub network, despite the fact that agents of the Satrap and King were both watching in every Nevada nightclub. He took a bus and saw someone suspicious get on behind him. Then he got off and boarded a bus going downtown, leaving the other man standing, and there, he got off and slipped into the foot traffic, went into a restaurant, walked into its restroom, and climbed out a window into the back alley. Later, he found the line of persons waiting to enter the Flames of Love, paid a couple of the partygoers to slip an envelope to one of the waiters with a tip. The message was simple:

> Delia, meet me at darkfall on the first full moon at the summit of the mountain of broken dreams.
>
> —Harold

He knew that Delia and only she would know the place, the very overlook where he had taken the scofflaw Viernes and her friends—a place where justice, in some measure at least, had won out against the impunity of wealth. It was indeed a place of broken dreams both for Viernes and for the girl she had killed, and their families.

For the next week, Harold dodged those seeking to track him. He left his assistants to manage his businesses for him. His only contact was a couple of calls from prepaid disposable cellular telephones. And thus, he bided his time. He stayed in random motels and paid cash he had drawn from ATMs all over town. In short, he did everything possible to avoid capture by his enemies. He was tortured by fears for his wife, but he realized that now that the King himself was involved, and now the Satrap had admitted he had her in his custody, Andrews had less chance to harm her at once. The King would want her trial and execution delayed until the time of Harold's, and that gave him a little delay. Eventually, the Satrap might arrange that she and Richard make a fatal try to escape, but to do that so soon after their capture would seem suspicious and was therefore unlikely. That's what Harold told himself in answer to his fears.

A full moon looked down on the winding road that led over the mountain from Kyle Canyon to Lee Canyon. Darkness had fallen half an hour ago. The shadows of the surrounding fir trees fell across the road. Millions of stars shown in the dark sky, but they could not be seen so perfectly because of the light that arose from the city that never sleeps—Las Vegas—spread across the valley below. In the distance, a solitary coyote howled at the moon, and moments later, others joined in.

Out of the darkness, a car appeared, an old beat-up rented Volkswagen pulled over on the overlook. Its lights went off and its motor stopped, and its driver waited. Half an hour later, the second car, a long dark limo, pulled up, and several dark figures emerged. Harold picked out the face of Delia easily because of his superior vision. The door of the other car opened, and Harold appeared.

"Delia, thank you for coming. We need to capture several of the Satrap's men to get one of them to talk. Only that way will I learn where he is holding my wife and child. Only that way will we be able to get a confession of treason."

"Your idea is a good one, Harold, but I think I can make it better. What if we capture Genevieve?"

"The Satrap's wife?" Harold said, just a little surprised that Delia would attack another woman, although he knew perfectly well of whom she spoke.

"Yes, if we can get her under our control, we will have a bargaining chip. Ronald loves his wife just as much as you love yours. The owner of the old Purple Sage Casino in Reno is going to hold a party to mark the twentieth anniversary of its opening. Genevieve worked there, first as a waitress and later as a stripper in one of its nightclubs."

"Wow, I knew she was an ex-waitress, but I never knew she had ever been a stripper," Harold remarked.

"If you are beautiful, it pays much better than being a waitress. And it affords good opportunities to meet wealthy men," she added.

"Or immortals," Harold suggested.

"Or immortals," Delia agreed. "The point is she will want to meet old friends who worked there in those days. Of course, she will be escorted by armed guards and at least some of the Satrap's vampires, she guessed. So it won't be an easy task to capture her."

"Yes," said Harold, "but it will also give us more persons to question, at least if we can capture them alive. Some of those people will also be human, the driver and the guards. We might even be able to read the minds of the mortals, but how much will they know about the conspiracy?" asked Harold

"Well, at least, Genevieve will know, and probably the vampires with her as well. That will give us a good chance to find out the details, and maybe even get confessions as well. Most important for you, Harold, is that the Satrap dare not hurt your wife while you hold his."

"Let's do it!" Harold said.

Genevieve's classic Chrysler 300 sedan was speeding through the Nevada night en route to Reno, passing along the silent roads through the desert. So far, the travelers had seen only a couple of vehicles, one of them a big semi-trailer truck, in the last hour. They had passed Indian Springs awhile back, and they just left Beatty. The occupants of the car were chatting sociably to pass the miles.

"It will be such fun to see the girls again. Some are still working as waitresses there, but most have graduated to management level positions or found husbands or lovers," Genevieve said addressing her vampire companions.

"I have heard that the girls working there now are just as pretty as they were back then," one was saying.

Suddenly, an ancient Ford Ranger truck pulled out partly blocking the road, in a place where dirt had been piled up on the shoulders and marked with orange cones and behind them a SUV pulled out. Someone threw out planks with spikes sticking up from them to complete the blocking of their retreat.

First, Harold's force took out two of the tires with gun fire. Then they fired tracer bursts over the truck. Red streaks flashing overhead revealed they had a lot of firepower.

"Surrender!" Harold demanded. "Surrender or die!"

The mortal guards threw down their weapons because they didn't want to die, but the vampire guards drew their swords and stepped out of the vehicle unconcerned about the gunfire, and full of fight, raising their weapons before them with both hands, as they made out some of their enemies in the darkness. A crossbow bolt tore through the first of them, not far from his heart. He looked down at the hole it made, then dropped his blade. The other did the same.

Quickly, Harold's men closed in and bound them with silver chains. Next, they handcuffed the mortals and chained

Genevieve's hands behind her. Then they bundled the lot of them into their own vehicles, cleared the road quickly, and took off.

Harold and Delia took turns questioning the prisoners. They worked on the mortals first because they are easier to read and less able to resist vampires. The two guards had been hired on contract from Jones's Security and knew nothing, but the driver, Julio Cesar, knew about the plot to install the Satrap as king after the murder of the existing Monarch. This was interesting but would not stand up as evidence because vampires can sway the minds of humans. The driver was to receive the gift of eternal life for his help.

The vampires would not tell anything, not even their names, but Harold and Delia suspected they knew all about the plot. Their very lives depended on their silence. Driver's licenses in their wallets identified the pair as Joseph Antonelli and Abraham Goldstien. Delia suspected that they had been criminals in their mortal lives before they were turned.

Harold telephoned the Satrap's house using a throw-away cellular. When the phone was picked up, he said, "I want to talk with Ronald Andrews."

"And you are?" with voice on the line asked.

"Harold Halbmann," he responded, and then moments later, he heard, "Andrews speaking."

"Listen, I have your wife and her guards as my prisoners. If you keep Cindy and Richard safe, they will also be safe."

"Listen, I would never hurt your wife or child."

"Nor will I hurt yours, but there must be no accident," Harold said.

"I wouldn't dream of it. Your Cindy and Richard are safe. Just keep Ginny safe too."

"I promise and my promise will be exactly as good as yours. Good-bye."

Genevieve pleaded her innocence of any plot against the Monarch, even after two hours of questioning. "There is no plot to harm our King," she said. "I can assure you also that Cindy and Richard are getting kind treatment."

In addition to her personal luggage, with her clothes and toiletries, the travelers had been carrying two briefcases. One of them, evidently belonging to Genevieve, was full of papers relating to a party planned at the Golden Cornucopia Hotel. There were guests lists, from which Delia, Harold, and Julia were absent of course, but including even some from other countries, there was a layout for the buffet, a wine list, and menu, contracts for the entertainers, dancers, singers, and musicians, and in fact, just about everything imaginable. There were also masters for the invitations some in English, some in Spanish.

The other briefcase had business information for the Satrap's enterprises in Northern Nevada. There was nothing proving treason that Harold or Delia could see on first examination.

Finally, Harold looked at the mess of papers and threw it back down on the table.

"Maybe Uncle Ernest can make something of this," he said. "He's the man of letters. I'm the man of action."

Meanwhile, Delia and Harold went back to work on the prisoners. No matter how hard they tried, they were not able to shake the two vampire guards or the Satrap's wife. They all knew their lives depended on their silence.

Ernest arrived two days later and began a careful examination of the papers taken from the Satrap's wife and her guards. He studied them for several hours and then laid them down to address Harold and Delia:

"There is evidence of treason in these papers although its stops short of being a slam dunk, as they say in basketball."

"What did you find?" Delia asked.

"You know that big party Genevieve is planning?"

"Yeah," said Harold, "what about it?"

"It's a reception for King Palaeologos XI. Now Archaelogos II, He Whose Name No Mortal May Speak, is our present monarch.

Palaeologos X was the last king. So just who is this new king, and why are they about to celebrate him in Nevada?"

"Unless…unless that is the title the usurper means to take," Harold said.

"One thing more, in the business reports, in the fine print, there is a reference to the need to turn thirty new vampires to support the King and there is a reference to a detailed order to accompany this. But I can't find that order, so where is it?" Ernest mused.

"That's too many newbies for any normal operation," Delia noted. "We're apex predators, and that is simply too many to turn at the same time."

"Let's fax the documents we have to Flames of Love and have the manager there give them to one of the King's agents," Harold suggested.

"Good idea," Delia concurred.

Two days later, when the King saw these papers, he was troubled. What did it mean that Genevieve was planning a party for another king? Was it treason, or were these documents fake? The Monarch found another name on one of the contracts, a party planner, Portia Beardsley.

"I want to talk with this woman at once," he told his secretary. "Have her brought here as soon as possible."

Although she was not unused to rooms like the glittering royal audience chamber—with its elevated throne, its walnut paneled walls, its chandelier and Persian carpet—Portia Beardsley, party planner to the Stars, was terrified when forced to her knees before the grim face of the immortal King.

The King got right to the point once they had brought her before him. Looking straight into her eyes, he asked, "Ms. Beardsley, look at this contract. Just who asked you to plan this party?"

"Genevieve Andrews requested me to do it. She said she wanted a party fit for a king for her husband."

The King observed there was no hint of deception in her face, the sound of her voice, or in her thoughts. The answer was plain truth.

"Who else knew about it?" the King asked.

"Well, lots of people. Several of her friends, her chauffer, and of course, all the people we were placing under contract."

The King decided he must take immediate action. Vampire kings who fail to follow up on charges of treason seldom reign long.

Next day, the vampire community in Nevada was stunned by news of the arrest and removal of the Satrap, his advisors, and the senior managers of all his businesses.

Just how wide does the web of the treasonable conspiracy extend? the King wondered. *Were Delia, Harold, and Julia involved at all, or were the charges against them only a smoke screen for the Satrap's treason?* The King pondered the question. *Hadn't Harold and those charged with treason brought these documents to his attention? Was that the action of traitors?* Still, he did not yet release Cindy and her son.

Meanwhile, Harold continued to grill his captives, especially Genevieve, to whom he gave considerable attention.

"Why did you and your husband try to have me killed and make me out as a traitor? What did I ever do to merit that kind of treatment?"

"I told him to leave you out of it, but my husband just couldn't accept that you wouldn't support his plans."

"Does he plan to kill our King and take over himself?"

"I didn't say that," she said. "I just described his attitude to you, that's all."

Harold couldn't get her to admit her treason, and he questioned the others, to no avail. No one wanted to admit being guilty of a capital crime.

Ernest had been studying the documents closely all the while, and now, he came forward considerably excited. "Look, Harold,

I've solved the mystery and found the missing paper. Let me show you this. It was behind the lining in the briefcase that had the business reports.

The paper asked the Nevada Satrap's northern representative to locate enough explosives from Nevada mining operations to build a bomb that would wipe out the King and his court. They wanted to pack the explosives into gift packages for the anniversary of the King's reign, two weeks from now. The plan also provided for raising enough new vampire warriors to seize power even if the explosion were less than entirely successful. They cannot fail. Harold faxed the incriminating papers to the same address used previously, confident that it would reach the King within a day or two.

When he traced how the detailed plan would work, the King quickly realized his suspicions were correct. Harold and his friends had absolutely nothing to do with the Satrap's plot. As it was there were plenty of conspirators at both ends of Nevada, enough to make major executions necessary to clear the state of treason. He would need Harold's help in reorganizing this shattered dominion, executing justice and restoring peace.

Delia, Harold, and Julia were summoned to appear before the throne of King Archaeologos II, He Whose Name No Mortal May Speak. The vampire prosecutor stood silent now, accusing no one at the moment.

They all bowed low before the most powerful immortal in the world.

"Delia of Delos, you are found innocent of all charges of treason. I couldn't believe that the mother of my line would turn against a child of her own children, and I was right. The charges were so serious, but the evidence supports your innocence. Julia Strange, you too are innocent. There has never been any killer in you, although you are an immortal, and like the rest of us must drink the blood of men. Harold Halbmann, Eternal Protector of the South, you too are innocent, and the charges against you were trumped up and ridiculous. We owe a special debt to you and to Delia for exposing the traitors to our reign. We find Richard Andrews, Genevieve Andrews, Harry Donaldson, Ernesto Mendez, John Samson, Maria Vazquez, Marion Albright, Samuel Smithson, Alice Johnson, Richard Towers, Samuel Cornwell, James Karp, and Marshall Patterson guilty of high treason as well as attempted murder and hereby sentence them to be staked out naked in the sun until dead.

"You, Harold Halbmann, we commission to carry the sentence into execution in accordance with the laws of the immortals. Execution of the sentence is to be complete within thirty days from this date. We also command you to review the circumstances of lesser followers and conspirators and to kill or free them in accord with our laws."

Harold left the audience chamber with a heavy heart because he did not want to become the King's executioner, but he was bound by law, and he knew any failure to carry out the royal instructions would mean a treason charge against him and Cindy, at least.

When he got to the Satrap's residence, Cindy sprang from the door and into his arms. They kissed with the fiery passion of those who have been freed from certain death. What a day it was, and what a night they would spend in each other's arms.

When they were alone together at last, after long absence, he took her in his arms, his lips sought hers and hers opened beneath his. He ran his hands over her, caressing her. He unbuttoned her blouse and gave her a playful nip. Then he reached behind her to release her bra and showered her breasts with kisses. Her fingers unbuttoned his shirt first, then opened his belt. Rapidly, they shed their remaining clothes and lay down together on the bed. As their excitement built, she opened her legs beneath him, he filled her, and thrust powerfully into her until the crescendo came and satisfied both after days of fear and long deprivation.

Next day, he visited the prisoners, who were housed in a converted warehouse, and read them the King's sentence. They could see any of their loved ones, and write wills if they wished, although most of their property belonged to the king. Harold said he would make an exception for small personal items. Most of them seemed stunned.

He and Cindy talked with Genevieve about her life, and her role in the conspiracy and her teenage daughter.

"Call me Ginny," she said. "I never wanted to involve you in this plot in any way. I told my husband to keep you out of it, but he just insisted in dragging you into this. I'm really sorry about it."

"So am I," Harold replied.

"I have had a good life," Genevieve added. "I'm just sorry it has to end this way. I have nothing I can leave my daughter even, except the memory of a foolish mother."

"There must have been some happy days once, Ginny," Cindy said.

"There were some good times—when I was young, when I worked at the Purple Sage with the girls and later, after he turned me, when Ronald and I married."

"Is your daughter from a previous relationship?" Cindy asked.

"Yes, Amanda. She's a fine young woman."

"Is her father still living?" Harold asked.

"I don't know and don't care. The creep got me into stripping, then deserted me as soon as I got pregnant." She paused a moment and then continued. "That turned out well though, because Ronald met me at that club."

That night, Harold and Cindy made love. They also reflected on the fact that things might have been much worse for them. They might have been in Ronald and Genevieve's shoes.

"Thank God for our deliverance," Harold said to which Cindy added her own "Amen."

Ronald and Genevieve spent hours together and at times seemed happy despite the shadow that hung over them both.

When they were together, it was as though both were in denial. They talked only of the happier days they had known together.

Twenty-seven days had run, and the time for Harold to complete the King's sentence was nearly at hand. Harold had continued to talk with the prisoners and to do whatever he could to help, although Ronald seemed unrepentant.

Marion Albright, a tall blond ex-showgirl, shared a cell with Maria Vazquez, a smaller black-haired Mexican vampire. Both were beautiful; both of them had been middle managers in Ronald's clubs. They were talking about their lives with Alice Johnson, a red-headed girl, smoking a cigarette in an adjacent cell.

Marion, remembering her showgirl days, suddenly chuckled. "At least, I won't have any bikini lines." But nobody else laughed. . . .

"I'm really hungry," Genevieve complained, her face too pale.

"It wouldn't be right to leave you that way," Harold declared.

He brought in the driver, Julio, who had known about the conspiracy, and pushed him protesting into Genevieve's cell.

"Drink deep and enjoy. I don't really care what you do with him," Harold said.

She was on him in a flash. Her fangs descended she tore open his throat and began to gulp down the blood. Harold wondered if she would drain him completely or not, but Genevieve stopped before the man's heart stopped beating, and she even closed his wounds with her tongue. Her color went back to normal. Harold had the driver removed, but he had lost too much blood and died later. He might have been saved if anyone had thought him worth turning.

"I know I have to die," Genevieve said. "I just wish I didn't have to bake to death slowly in the sun. I'm terrified to suffer that way."

"Ginny, I have no choice but to execute the King's command and to follow the dictates of immortal law. Ask me for anything else."

"Please, an easier death," she pleaded. "Please help me."

Harold's heart was moved. He had confirmed from others that she had indeed tried to keep him out of this mess.

Harold thought about it, and he ordered a heavy plank, cut in segments and slotted, so it could be fitted together to form an H, the center member forming the block. He found a suitable room at the old warehouse, and he covered the floor with black plastic sheets. He placed the block close to one end, brought in an ax with a broad blade, and leaned it against the wall. Four hours before it was time for him to kill the prisoners, he went to Genevieve's cell.

"Please," she pleaded again. "I don't want to cook to death. Find another way for me."

"Ginny, the King has commanded you to be exposed to the sun, but I can make it so it won't hurt at all."

"How?" she asked, and relief showed all over her face. "How will you do that?"

"If you are already dead, then it can't hurt," Harold said. "A single stroke of the ax and you'll suffer no more pain. Come then, and let's end this agony," he said, holding out his hand. She started to take it, then hesitated.

"It's an easier way," Harold said.

"I know, and I am very, very afraid of roasting alive. I keep thinking of poor Ronald though, dying alone, cursed even by his own followers. I just can't do that to him, at least one person who cares for him should see him through to the end." She hesitated a moment.

"But,... at the execution, can you stake me out beside him?"

"Of course," Harold said, "if you are really willing to die that death."

She looked at him for a long moment, with a glance that seemed to show wavering resolve. "A wife should stick with her husband to the bitter end. I might have been a queen. Now we only have death to share."

Harold closed and secured the cell door. "Good-bye for now," he said

V. FINAL JUSTICE

At the appointed time, Harold and his men loaded the prisoners into two large vans and drove into the desert night. When they reached the place, they all got out. They took each of the condemned men one by one and stripped every stitch of clothing off, and they made the women undress completely. Each man was staked out, spread-eagled, and faced toward the sky. Each woman was staked out, spread-eagled, and faced toward the earth.

Three vampire men had been staked out; the rest of the condemned, hands bound behind them huddled together in a protective mass, shivering, watching, and waiting, surrounded by guards in the darkness.

"Marion Albright, it's your turn."

Reluctantly, Marion walked out of the mass and advanced a few paces. A guard stepped behind her and released the chain holding her hands.

"Strip," the voice demanded, "everything."

Marion unbuttoned her blouse and dropped it to the ground. Then she peeled her slacks off and stepped out of them. Next, she reached behind her back to unfasten her bra and drop it to the earth also. She knew she would never need clothes again—this was it. She must have seemed to hesitate a moment.

"Thong too," the voice demanded.

She pushed it down with her thumbs and then stepped out of it. She crossed her arms over her breasts, shivering in the predawn chill.

A guard pointed to a direction. "Over there," he said. Marion walked over.

"Stretch out on your belly and extend your hands and feet."

She lay down on the sandy soil as directed, and hands seized and fettered her hands, stretching them out at a forty-five-degree angle. They pulled off her shoes and socks and fettered her feet drawing them apart at a forty-five-degree angle. Then she heard the mallet pounding in the stakes. But her mind went elsewhere. *When the burning starts*, she thought, *I will keep silent as long as I can. I don't want the bastards to hear my screams. Perhaps the others will drown mine out.*

Then, they were finished with Marion.

"Maria Vazquez, it's your turn," the voice said.

The petite Mexican girl stepped out of the mass of the condemned, and a guard released her hands.

"Strip," the voice commanded, "all your clothes off."

In moments, her top, shorts, bra, and panties made a sad little pile on the ground.

"Over there, hurry up."

She ran to where the guard was pointing.

"On your belly, now."

She stretched out, and quickly, they stripped off her shoes and socks and staked her out spread-eagled beside Marion. Then, they were done with Maria.

"Richard Towers, it's your turn."

Richard, trembling with fear, emerged from the others.

Two guards seized him by the arms, and half-lifted, half-dragged him to the place where he would be stripped and staked, the place he would die. . . .

Ronald Andrews stood defiantly, his hands bound behind him beside his wife, Genevieve, whose hands were also secured behind her back, alone now where all the condemned had been. They were the last ones.

"Ronald Andrews, it's your turn now."

Ronald strode forward a few steps, and then two powerful vampires seized him and conducted him to the place where they had determined he should die. Each inserted an arm under one of his and wrapped a leg around his, immobilizing him totally. A third guard opened his belt buckle and jerked his trousers and undershorts down, only slightly more brutally than with the rest of the male vampires, exposing him. Then the guard unfastened his hands, so they could strip off his shirt and undershirt, and he screamed out as the last of his garments were being pulled off.

"Harold, I should have killed you rather than ask you to support me, you SOB!"

"That's exactly right," Harold said calmly.

They pushed Ronald and dropped him on his back, on the sandy ground, then splayed his arms and legs out to a forty-five-degree angle, took off his shoes and socks, and staked him out for the rising sun. They were done with him.

"Ginny," Harold said, "I'm sorry, but it's your turn now."

Genevieve walked two dozen steps forward towards Harold, who stepped behind her to unfasten the chain that bound her hands.

"Undress completely," he commanded.

She unbuttoned her blouse and dropped it from her shoulders, unfastened her slacks, bent to push them down, and then stepped out of them. She unhooked and dropped her bra and then pushed down and stepped out of her panties.

"We are going over there, where the four men are standing. That is where your husband is. Let's get this finished."

Genevieve walked quickly over, and Harold followed behind her. She hesitated and trembled a moment when she saw her husband staked out naked on the ground.

"There." A guard pointed at a patch of earth.

"On your belly, Ginny," Harold ordered.

She fell to her knees and then lay down.

"Stretch out your arms and legs."

When she did that, the guards seized and fettered her hands, stripped off her shoes and socks, fettered her ankles, spread-eagled her, and chained her to the stakes. Rapid hammer blows drove in the four stakes. And then, they were done with Genevieve, staked out beside her husband according to vampire law.

Ronald turned his head and looked over and saw his wife, the wife he had loved, the wife who would have to suffer terrible final agony with him, and then he said, "I'm so sorry, Ginny, that you have to die this way with me. You would have been my queen, but we gambled and lost."

"I love you," she said. "I'm sorry we had to end up this way."

Harold realized that Ronald would never know that his wife had given up an easy death and embraced hideous suffering just because she wanted to share life with him to the very end.

"Ronald, you bastard!" one of the condemned shouted. "All of us have to die because of you."

"Shut up," another voice called out. "It's the damn King who is killing us, not Ronald."

For the moment, the rest remained silent.

The crews gathered up the clothing that would no longer be needed by the condemned from the ground, nine shirts, nine pairs of slacks, six T-shirts, three men's undershirts, seven pairs of boxer shorts and two of briefs, and nine pairs of shoes and socks from the men, and from the women, one dress and slip, two blouses, two pairs of slacks, one woman's top, one pair of short shorts, four bras, three panties and a thong, and four pairs of socks, three of shoes, one pair of sandals. They stuffed them into six garbage bags, one for men's outer garments, one for men's underclothes and socks, one for men's shoes, one for women's outerwear, one for their underclothes and socks, and one for their shoes.

Then Harold and his men then withdrew out of earshot to a place where they could make sure nobody came onto the scene. None wanted to hear the cries of the condemned at first burn, the useless pleading, the curses against the King or prayers, the screams of pain of the sizzling, or the groans and moans of the charred and dying. The sun would break over the horizon in twenty minutes. By evening, all the condemned would be dead, every one of them burned black. Just as she had foretold, there would be no bikini lines on Marion Albright's charred flesh.

Harold went straight home leaving others to guard the site; he had had enough of killing.

My mother had to die that way, he remembered. *May God have mercy on them all, especially on Ginny.*

VI. A Change of Government in Nevada

Harold was dreading the news when it came. He had always wanted to avoid vampire politics and live quietly with his wife Cindy, his son Richard and to enjoy his friendships with Delia, Julia and other members of the immortal and human community. Instead a special messenger from the King brought him a parchment document. He looked at it but he could not read the words, he needed Uncle Ernest. After Uncle Ernest examined the parchment he read the words aloud.

> We, Archeologos II, We Whose Name No Mortal May Speak, to our trusted and well-beloved vassal Harold Santiago, called Halbmann, Eternal Protector of the Southern Realm, and to all to whom these presents shall come, greetings, and the gift of life eternal.
>
> We appoint Harold as Satrap of Nevada, and as such grant him royal power while he shall continue in office. Within the State of Nevada and throughout its lands, he shall command for me. Whoever obeys him, obeys me.
>
> Whoever shall raise his hand against his satrap raises it against me also. Therefore, all are commanded to obey him as if he were me.
>
> He manages the royal patrimony within his State, collects whatever is due to me, and distributes funds to our servants.
>
> He hears cases and does justice for us, having the power of life and death.
>
> Given this second day August of the twelfth year of our reign under our hand and seal. Witnessed by Shane Richards our State Secretary.

Harold noticed there was a large red wax seal attached to the document by cords, certifying its authenticity. This was something he never wanted, crushing responsibility, with the possibility that some ambitious person would seize on the slightest slip up to replace him in the favor of the King, and surely costing him and Cindy their lives. The document was published to the Nevada Vampires and all of them pledged their fealty.

His first task Harold knew had to be to deal with the last of the conspirators. Here he needed to tread a fine line, if he spared too many, the King might read some treason into his actions, but he also didn't want to begin his new government as a butcher.

Harold assembled his council in the very chamber where the old one had met to condemn him, Delia, and Julia. This time, however, all of them would be present at the meeting as were Ernest Frank and representatives from every vampire business or operation in the state.

"Our first business is to clear our community of the last elements of treason, at the same time rehabilitating the lives of some of their supporters when they no longer constitute a danger to the King or to our community.

"I believe that the vampires who were accompanying Genevieve to the Purple Sage Hotel in Reno, Joseph Antonelli and Abraham Goldstein must die because they knew of Ronald's treason. We also have Rick Conrad, Michael Hancock, and David Larson, personal advisors of the old Satrap, and they too should perish according to our laws. There are also three more managers from Ronald's operations in the Reno area—Hector Fischer, Kate Buckley, and Raymond Wilson who were preparing the bomb to use against our King, and Robert Howarth, Betty Jones, Mary Evans, and Sally Jaffe, who were recruiting vampire warriors for the Satrap's army, and so are guilty of capital crimes. Now as for the two mortal guards who accompanied Genevieve, they were hired from a security company, and there is no evidence they knew anything, so we will mesmerize them and release them. They won't lose anything more than their jobs for an unexplained absence.

"Now if anyone has any evidence whatsoever to support the innocence of any of those I mentioned who I believe merit death, I will hear it carefully. The last thing I want is to harm any person who is not guilty. I will also consider any evidence that any of the accused would no longer be a threat to our community, but it will have to be very, very strong to sway me.

"All persons who worked for the late Satrap who fall under the third rank of responsibility I will save, if they will pledge their loyalty to our King and to me, personally, and if so, they can remain in their present employments. Relatives and friends of the conspirators who might have known, or guessed that there was a conspiracy, but who had no active role, I pardon also. What does the council think of my list?"

Delia then rose to speak about the list, hesitated a moment, and then began. "I know some of the accused, and I find it difficult to believe that they would have done such horrible things, but it seems to me the evidence supports their guilt."

"Would it violate immortal law to allow the accused to answer the charges?" Ernest inquired. "It seems to me that the King has granted you broad authority, and some things, perhaps even this, are at your discretion."

Julia thought that would be a good idea too. "Courts throughout the mortal world allow for a defense. If you have full powers here, why not set a precedent."

A few grumbled that that would change the way vampires had always done justice, but in the end, most council members favored the idea.

When the accused had all been assembled in Las Vegas, they were divided into groups, each of which was brought before Harold to be heard. The first two were Joe Antonelli and Abe Goldstein. Timothy Kopp, from Flames of Love, acted as prosecutor.

"Joseph Antonelli and Abraham Goldstein were confidants of the late Satrap and were present at meetings where his treason was certainly discussed. They supported their boss in his actions against those he was persecuting. They were criminals in their mortal lives, but far more important, they are traitors worthy of death."

"Do either of you wish to offer evidence in your own defense?" Harold asked. "If you know anyone who can refute these charges, say only his name, and I will summon him to testify."

The response was defiant silence. So after a few moments, Harold continued. "Since you stand mute, under the authority vested in me by our King, I sentence you to be taken to the place of execution, stripped naked, and staked out for the sun until you are dead, in accordance with immortal law and custom. Sentence will be executed thirty days from this date."

The Satrap's advisors had attended almost every meeting of his council as recorded by the register. They offered no defense, and Harold condemned them too.

Next, they brought in those who were accused of building the bomb for assassinating the King. Unfortunately for them, their names were found in the paper that Ernest had discovered, something they could not deny. Harold sentenced them to death also.

Finally, Harold dealt with those charged with recruiting and turning soldiers for the usurper's vampire army. The names of Richard Howarth and Betty Jones were also on documents about turning new warriors for the Satrap, and Mary Evans and Sally Jaffe were listed as assigned to this task, so the evidence pointed to their guilt too.

"We were not told anything about raising troops for anyone," Sally protested. "Richard just told me and Mary to seduce and turn some big, strong, young men, so we did. We had no idea it was connected to a plot against the King."

"Does Sally speak the truth, Richard?" Harold asked.

"Yes, that's right," he said.

"Betty," Harold inquired, "is that right?"

"That's the way it happened. I didn't tell Mary until later."

"Did Sally ever know?'

"Never," Betty said. "She's too much of a talker. I wouldn't trust her to keep her mouth shut. Anyway, she had no need to know."

"Richard, is that right? Did you ever tell Sally?"

"Never," he said.

Harold thought about it. *Maybe they were only trying to save a friend, but vampire males asked females to do things often enough without explaining why. Also, Betty's comments about why she didn't want to tell Sally seemed right.* He was ready then to render a verdict.

"Sally Jaffe, there is reasonable doubt as to your guilt. Therefore, I release you. Richard Howath, Betty Jones, and Mary Evans, under the authority vested in me by our King, I sentence you to be taken to the place of execution, stripped naked, and staked out for the sun until you are dead, in accordance with immortal law and custom. Sentence will be executed thirty days from this date."

Harold ordered that until it was time to die the prisoners would be treated with every kindness. They could receive visitors and chat with friends, write letters, draw up their wills. Nor did he forget the unfortunate Genevieve. Each immortal prisoner was to be given a cup of freshly drawn human blood once every week. Some felt Harold was too kind to these criminals, but he remained firm in his resolution.

When the time drew close, Harold called in Timothy Kopp and Edwin Minehain, his assistant, who were to take charge execution of the sentence. Harold explained how he wanted them to do it.

"Follow immortal law strictly, but with no additional cruelty. I don't want to have anyone spraying water into the mouths of the condemned at first burn to delay onset of the sizzle, and I certainly don't want anyone to spray water in their mouths and on their backs when they are sizzling in order to prolong their agony. In fact, I don't even want anyone in earshot of them while they are dying."

"Do you understand my instructions?" Harold asked.

"Yes," they both said, but then Edwin added, "I think you are losing an opportunity here. Certainly, we need human help to get the most out of them, but that's not too hard to do. To begin with, during the first burn, when they start to beg, many criminals will blurt out confessions that make our case against them stronger, or else they may offer the names of other conspirators. It's amazing what a little water and the desire to postpone the inevitable will do.

"During the first two and a half hours of full sun, the first burn, they can repair part of the damage but become more and more dehydrated. They are still coherent, although in increasing pain, and a little water can extend the time to a full three and a half hours. Because their faces are not exposed fully under the sun, the females last a little longer and are still able to talk right into the start of the sizzle when the flesh begins to burn. They are in agony, but they usually go crazy when their hair bursts into flame. Spraying a little water on their hair and back, as well as their mouth, can keep them conscious and coherent through the fourth hour, and maybe just a bit more. They can still tell us things."

"First of all," Harold said, "we don't need any confessions. If we aren't sure a person is guilty, we have no business staking him out. Second, the condemned would offer anyone's name, even yours, for a few moments of relief, so that evidence, the evidence of torture, is worthless. Carry out the execution exactly in accordance with my instructions. That is one of those cases where less kindness really ends up being more. I want each of the condemned to have the quickest death immortal laws allow."

Thus, it was that thirty days after Harold's verdict Tim Kopp and Harold's men loaded twelve condemned vampires into two

Ford wagons, drove out into the Nevada night, unloaded them at the place of execution, stripped them naked, and staked them for the morning sun. After staking them out, one of the crew recalled that Mary Evans turned her head to look at Betty Jones, staked out beside her, and said, "Why in the hell did to you have to be so damn honest?" Then the stakeout squad left, and the blazing sun rose and made an end to Ronald Andrew's conspiracy against the King of all Vampires.

VII. A New Day Dawns

A few days later Ernest was talking to a man in the Coffee Shop at the Golden Cornucopia. This fellow was a researcher from Nevada University which had almost recovered from the damage inflicted on it by Nevada's vampire governor. He was having his lunch on break from his work. Ernest had noticed his white lab coat, which stimulated his curiosity.

"We are doing some fantastic research on blood and plasma he said. Dr. Robert Dean thinks it may soon be possible to produce an almost completely artificial blood substitute using just a bit of plasma. The new substitute could be stored for much longer periods for issue in case of emergencies, such as wars or natural disasters, he said.

"We do need to get grants, and our University was seriously hurt by cuts in funding during the Santiago administration. Oh, by the way I'm Samuel Richards, a lab assistant over there."

"You know, I happen to know one of the wealthiest business men in town," Ernest said. "Maybe you have heard of Harold Halbmann. You may remember him from the TV ads for Halbmann Motors or Halbmann Enterprises, his umbrella corporation. He would be very interested in Dr. Dean's work, and he has deep pockets."

Thus it was that a casual meeting, an accidental encounter, led to the foundation of one of the most significant research efforts in human and in vampire history. Sam happened to mention Harold to Dr. Dean, right after his request for an important research grant was turned down, by people who didn't think anything worthwhile could come from a cow country college like Nevada University.

Dr. Dean talked with Harold about money, and Harold said he thought he could help secure the cash, and then he talked of the need for securing blood donations for research and other use. That really excited Harold who had some ideas of his own.

"You we could organize a new corporation, with a name such as Bloodcentric to carry on your research. You know we can offer all donors free blood testing for life and send the tests to any doctor who needs them. We will need to test donor's blood anyway, and by providing a little medical help, we may help unlock the generosity of donors."

"That's a splendid idea," Doctor Dean declared. "How soon can we get the money and organize the company?"

So that is how Bloodcentric was born, and within seven years of its birth, the mere batting of an eyelash from vampire perspective, the company began trials of a new blood product which they called Permablood. Now Permablood was not really permanent, but it had a shelf life ten times longer that existing plasma, and it was way better too.

The Nevada vampire community became excited first, and then the news flashed through the immortal community around the world. The King even sent a letter, congratulating Harold for his good work and asking for more details about the research.

"Well done, my good and trusty vassal. Harold, your accomplishments never cease to amaze me, and your services to the immortal world are outstanding. How soon will the new product be available to all of us? Give my regards to Dr. Dean, and tell him one good turn deserves another. Keep me posted on this product's development, please!"

Vampires, of course, became major beneficiaries of the Permablood revolution, but even while research was advancing part of the blood donations were used for vampires, the rest was sent to hospitals or used in the research.

Permablood incorporated elements of real human blood serum along with the artificially made compound. The two were blended to produce the new product. Nor did Bloodcentric research stop with the original blood substitute. Harold and Doctor Dean wanted it to have a longer and longer shelf life. Permablood also helped humankind, just as the doctor had intended from the first, so here were two different races gaining from science.

Dr. Dean began to age with the years, but finally, he accepted the gift of eternal life from Harold, for only in this way would he be able to continue his research forever. Perhaps it was Delia who best explained the long-term results of his new discoveries to the Satrap's council.

"Vampires or immortals, whatever you want to call us, have always been apex predators. Thus, our population always has had to be considerably smaller than that of humanity, which supplies us with the sustenance of life. Dr. Dean's discoveries open the possibility of a world that could support a larger number of vampires without any damage at all to the human race. They hasten the day when vampires and men may live openly and peacefully side by side, each benefiting from the achievements of the other."

Quickly Bloodcentric organized donation centers and a distribution system for Permablood throughout the nation and, very soon afterward, on a world-wide basis. The operations of this company meant millions of dollars to the community and to Nevada. The operations were so successful that people even wanted to buy up houses in Las Vegas's long abandoned suburbs and demanded restoration of normal power, water, sewer, and trash services in formerly abandoned parts of town.

Harold handled the tedious details of his new administration amazingly well, but that may have been true partly because of his business experience. Of course, it was Ernest Frank who reviewed contracts and written documents for him. At least when he couldn't put them in an autoreader that scanned the written text and read it aloud. Equipment that would work with Latin texts might exist in the highest levels of the Roman Catholic Church, but Harold couldn't get his hands on it. Delia and Julia also helped him in different ways. Delia's experience in handling nightclub operations was a key to managing the most profitable of the Vegas vampires' operations. He also sent her north where she looked over, organized, and revised the operations that Ronald had set up there. Julia was Harold's conscience always reminding him of the need to treat others with all the kindness possible. Also, she developed more and more ability to really understand every kind of human heart.

Harold's greatest joy came from his love for his wife Cindy, and he really understood Ronald's last words to his wife. Harold loved Cindy so much, and he trembled to think of what it might have been like, of the horror he would have felt, if it had been he and Cindy who had been staked out to die that terrible death. He feared vampire politics with its awful violence and arbitrary deeds. He resolved firmly that he would do everything in his power to soften that, to bring the best government possible to Nevada's immortals.

Harold also remembered Elmer David, the brave human who had faced up to the power of a monstrous vampire and paid with his life for his courageous stand. Harold continued to pay David's salary to his widow every month on schedule. As for David's children, each one received a full scholarship to Nevada University. The eldest chose to attend graduate school, and a mysterious donor paid his way in full. Later, he rose to a managerial position in the Reno hotel industry. The other child married soon after graduation and received a brand-new car from Halbmann Motors.

Then there was Richard growing and maturing every day, full of questions about his world, a world where he too was destined to be a powerful immortal. Harold would always remember that day when he had been speaking of Delia and her children, and the many things they had done that Richard asked him. "What's a line, Dad, and what exactly does lineage mean?"

"We immortals have two kinds of children, son. Some are like you, born from the seed of a father and egg of a mother. Others are different."

"How are they different?" Richard wanted to know

"Well, these children begin as humans, a slightly different species. When we share our blood with them, we become part of them. Our blood replaces what was before, thus we become part of them, and they are our children.

"Both natural children and those made from humans are part of our line, and from them come other children, who carry our lineage. In time, it becomes difficult to trace them all down.

Delia, for example, is that old. But the King is of her lineage, and that is a powerful protection for all her friends. You know what," Harold said to the young man standing before him, and he looked over at Cindy seated beside him on the couch with a sparkle in his eyes and smiled. "It will soon be time for us to give you a new sister. It will be awhile, but that time will come before you know it." He put his arm around her.

"Yeah, let's go for it," she said, looking into his eyes.

Ernest sat at his *scriptorium*, and he dipped the quill into the lamp black ink, and wrote smoothly, his pen running over the page. He told about all these deeds in Latin, and finished the first part: *Sic post mortes satrapis Ronaldi atque uxoris ejus, Harolus factus est Satrapes Civitatis Nivatae.* "And thus after the deaths of Ronald

and his wife, Harold was made satrap of the State of Nevada."
Aurora est novae aetatis. "It is," he wrote, "the dawn of a new age."
Then he began to describe a new age that had just begun.

CPSIA information can be obtained at www.ICGtesting.com
Printed in the USA
LVOW04s1241020415

432955LV00020B/473/P

9 781631 226434